Praise for Ed McBain & the 87th Precinct

"Raw and realistic...The bad guys are very bad, and the good guys are better." —*Detroit Free Press*

"Ed McBain's 87th Precinct series...simply the best police procedurals being written in the United States." —*Washington Post*

"The best crime writer in the business." —*Houston Post*

"Ed McBain is a national treasure." —*Mystery News*

"It's hard to think of anyone better at what he does. In fact, it's impossible."—Robert B. Parker

"I never read Ed McBain without the awful thought that I still have a lot to learn. And when you think you're catching up, he gets better."
—Tony Hillerman

"McBain is the unquestioned king...light years ahead of anyone else in the field." —*San Diego Union-Tribune*

"McBain tells great stories." —Elmore Leonard

"Pure prose poetry...It is such writers as McBain who bring the great American urban mythology to life." —*The London Times*

"The McBain stamp: sharp dialogue and crisp plotting."
—*Miami Herald*

"You'll be engrossed by McBain's fast, lean prose." —*Chicago Tribune*

"McBain redefines the American police novel...he can stop you dead in your tracks with a line of dialogue." —*Cleveland Plain Dealer*

"The wit, the pacing, his relish for the drama of human diversity [are] what you remember about McBain novels." —*Philadelphia Inquirer*

"McBain is a top pro, at the top of his game." —*Los Angeles Daily News*

THE CON MAN

THE CON MAN

AN 87TH PRECINCT NOVEL

ED McBAIN

THOMAS & MERCER

The characters and events portrayed in this book are fictitious. Any similarity to real persons, living or dead, is coincidental and not intended by the author.

Printed in the United States of America.

Published by Thomas & Mercer
P.O. Box 400818
Las Vegas, NV 89140

ISBN-13: 9781612181844
ISBN-10: 1612181848

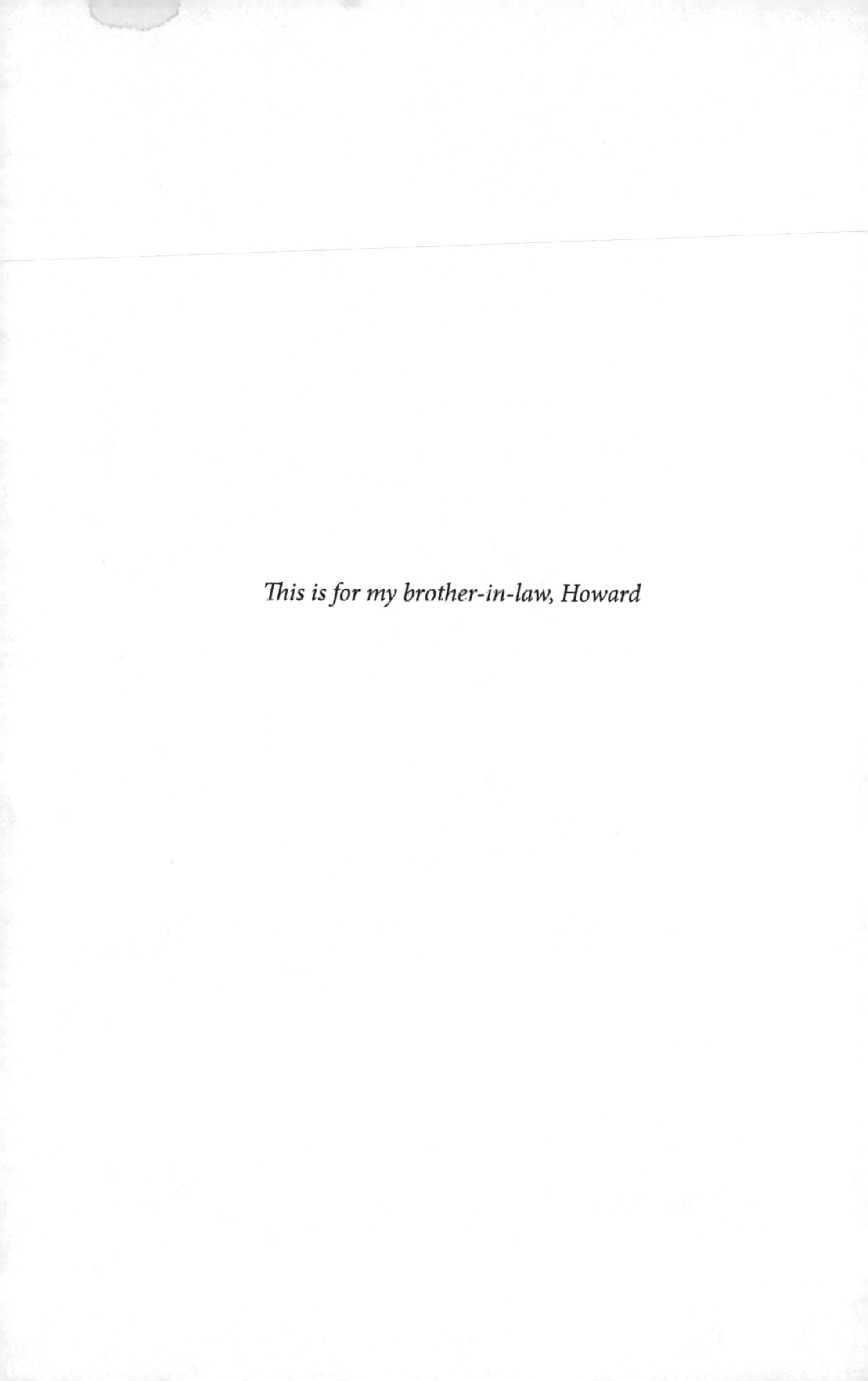

This is for my brother-in-law, Howard

The city in these pages is imaginary.
The people, the places are all fictitious.
Only the police routine is based on established
investigatory technique.

Everybody has a right to earn a living.

That's the American way. You get out there and sweat, and you make a buck. And you invest that buck in lemons and sugar. The water and ice, you get free. You've got yourself a little lemonade stand by the side of the road, and pretty soon, you're pulling in five bucks a week. You take that five, and you buy more lemons and more sugar, and you spot your stands at intervals along the road, and pretty soon, you can't handle all the business. You hire people to work for you. You start putting the lemonade up in bottles and then cans, and before you know it, you're freezing the stuff, and it's being distributed in chain stores all over the country. You buy yourself a big house in the country with a swimming pool and a garbage disposal unit, and you go to cocktail parties where people serve your lemonade with a little bit of gin tossed in for kicks. You have arrived in spades.

That's the American way, and everybody has a right to earn a living.

The law doesn't quarrel with man's inalienable right to pursue the buck. The law only questions the method and means of acquiring the elusive green.

If, for example, your particular penchant is cracking safes, the law may cock a slightly disciplinary eyebrow in your direction.

Or if, for example, you like to hit people on the head and take their wallets, you can't very well blame the law for looking at you somewhat disdainfully.

Or if, to stretch a point, you make your living by hiring out a gun, *your* gun, by squeezing the trigger of that gun, by using that gun to actually shoot people—well, really!

You can, after all, be a gentleman about all this. You can, if you figure crime is the quickest, safest, most exciting way of making the most money in the shortest time, go about it like a gent.

You can fool people.

You need not resort to violence.

You need not go out and buy a costly set of burglars' tools.

You need not acquire a pistol.

You need not draw up complicated plans for getting in and out of a bank.

You need not set up an expensive counterfeit printing press in your basement.

You can remain a gentleman, pursue a life of romantic criminal adventure, see the world, meet a lot of nice people, drink a lot of cool drinks, and still make a lot of money—all by fooling people.

You can, in short, become a con man.

The little Negro girl was very nervous. She was nervous because she was in a police station talking to two detectives. One of the detectives was Negro, too, but that didn't make her any less nervous. Both detectives were listening to her sympathetically, but that didn't make her feel any less a fool—and she supposed this feeling of foolishness was what made her feel so nervous.

She had been in the city for two years now. She had come up from North Carolina a long while ago, and she knew she'd looked green at the time, and she knew her speech was not Northern, but that was a long time ago, and she'd thought she was quite cosmopolitan by now, quite the city slicker. Pride goeth before a fall, she supposed, and she sat with her foolishness inside her, and her nervousness breaking out on her hands, which picked lint from the small black purse she carried.

She sat in the detective squadroom of the 87th Precinct on a mild day in April. There had been rain just a little while before, and the greenery in Grover Park across the street had shoved its clean, sweet scent onto the air, and the cleanness and sweetness had somehow managed to cross the street and filter in through the grilled windows of the squadroom. The squadroom did not very often smell sweet. The squadroom housed sixteen detectives who, while they were not always all there at the same time, worked hard nonetheless in somewhat cramped quarters. Detectives sweat. That sounds almost sacrilegious because everyone knows only *living* human beings sweat. But even admitting that some detectives aren't quite human, let's be kind and allow that some of them are almost quite living. Which is why the sweet smell from the park was a welcome one on that April day, which had miraculously turned to one of sunshine after a bad start.

"I feel awful silly about this," the girl said.

"What was your name again, miss?" Kling asked. Kling was a detective/3rd grade. He was tall and blond and somewhat young looking, mainly because he *was* young. He was the newest detective on the squad, and sometimes, his questions weren't exactly to the point because he was still learning the art of questioning. Sometimes, too, his questions made him feel a little foolish. So Bert Kling knew just how the young Negro girl in the straight-back chair felt.

"My name is Betty," she said. "Betty Prescott."

"Where do you live, Betty?" Kling asked.

"Well, I work for some people in the next state. I'm a domestic, you know? I been working for them for six months now. Mr. and Mrs. Haines?" She made the last a question, and she raised her eyebrows as if expecting Kling to know who Mr. and Mrs. Haines were. Kling did not know. "I'm supposed to be back there now," Betty said. "Thursday's my day off, you see. Thursdays and every other Sunday. I generally come into the city every Thursday. Mr. Haines drives me to the station, and then Mrs. Haines picks me up when I come back. I'm supposed to be back now, but I felt I should report this. I called Mrs. Haines, and she said, by all means, I should report it. You see?"

"I see," Kling said. "Do you keep an apartment in the city?"

"I live with my cousin here. Isabel Johnson?" Again she made the name a question. Kling didn't know Isabel Johnson, either.

"All right, what happened, Betty?" Brown asked. He had been silent up to this point, giving Kling his head. But Arthur Brown was a detective/2nd grade and a known tendency toward impatience. He was impatient, perhaps, because his name was Brown and the accidentals of birth had tinted his complexion the same color. He had taken a lot of ribbing from fellow Americans over the years and had once considered changing his name to Lipschitz so that the hate mongers could really have a ball. His impatience, as it related to his chosen profession, was sometimes a hindrance, but it crossed a very subtle line into a second character trait, and that trait was doggedness. Once Brown got his teeth into a case, he wouldn't unclamp his jaws until the nut was cracked. His impatience was a peculiar thing. There was, for example, a detective named Meyer Meyer at the precinct. Meyer's surname was, of course, Meyer, and Meyer's father had stuck him with the given name of Meyer so that his offspring emerged as Meyer Meyer. Now, if ever a man took guff because of a handle some unthinking parent had given him, Meyer Meyer was that man. But, in Meyer, the years of guff had led to an almost supernatural attitude of patience. The only crack in Meyer's veneer of extreme patience emerged in a physical way. For Meyer Meyer was as bald as a cue ball, even though he was a young man. But that's the way it goes. Two men, two names, two extremes.

Impatiently, Brown asked, "What happened?"

"I got off the train yesterday morning," Betty said. "I take the eight-seventeen in with Mr. Haines. I don't sit with him because he's always talking business with his friends. He's in public relations?" Again, the question mark. Kling nodded.

"Go on," Brown said impatiently.

"Well, when we got here to the city, I got off the train, and I was walking along when this man came up to me."

"Where was this?" Brown asked.

"Right in the station," Betty said.

"Go ahead."

"He said hello, and he asked me was I new in the city? I said, no, I'd been up North for two years, but I was working out the state. He seemed like a very nice fellow, dressed nice, you know? Respectable?"

"Yes," Kling said.

"Anyway, he said he was a preacher. He looked like a preacher, too. He started blessing me then. He said God bless you and all like that, and he said I should be very careful in the big city because there was all kinds of pitfalls for a young, innocent girl. People who'd want to do me harm?"

Again, the question mark, and again, Kling said, "Yes," and immediately afterwards cursed himself for falling into the pitfall of the girl's speech pattern.

"He said I should be especially careful with money, because there was all sorts of people who'd do most anything to get their hands on it. He asked me if I had any money with me."

"Was he white or Negro?" Brown asked.

Betty looked at Kling somewhat apologetically. "He was white," she said.

"Go ahead," Brown told her.

"Well, I said I had a little money with me, and he asked me if I'd like him to bless it for me? He said, 'Do you have a ten-dollar bill,' and I said no. So he said, 'Do you have a five-dollar bill,' and I said yes. Then he took out his own five-dollar bill, and he put it into this little white envelope. With a cross on the front. A crucifix?"

This time Kling did not say yes. He did not even nod.

"Then he said something like, 'God bless this money and keep it safe from those who would…' Oh, like that. We kept talking, and he put the envelope back in his pocket, and then he said, 'Here, my child, you take this blessed five dollars and let me have your bill.' I gave him my five dollars, and he reached into his pocket and gave me the envelope with the cross on it, the envelope with the blessed money."

"And this morning?" Brown asked impatiently.

"Well, this morning I was ready to go to the train station, and I saw the envelope in my purse, so I opened it up?"

"Yes," Kling said.

"Surprise," Brown said. "No five dollars."

"Why, no!" Betty said. "There was just a folded paper napkin in the envelope. He must have switched that envelope while he was talking to me, after he'd blessed the money. I don't know what I'm going to do now. I needed that five dollars. Can't you catch him?"

"We'll try," Kling said. "Can you give us a description of the man?"

"Well, I didn't really look at him too hard. He was nice looking and very nicely dressed?"

"What was he wearing?"

"A dark-blue suit. Or maybe black. It was dark, anyway."

"Tie?"

"A bow tie, I think."

"Carrying a briefcase or anything?"

"No."

"Where'd he get the envelope from?"

"His inside pocket."

"Did he tell you his name?"

"If he did, I don't remember."

"All right, Miss Prescott," Brown said, "if anything develops, we'll call you. In the meantime, I think you'd better forget all about that five dollars."

"*Forget* it?" she asked with a great big question mark, and nobody answered her.

They led her to the slatted wooden railing that divided the squadroom from the corridor outside, and they watched her walk down the corridor and then turn into the stairwell that led to the ground floor of the building.

"What do you think?" Kling asked Brown.

"The old switch game," Brown said. "There are a hundred variations. We'd better plant a few men at the station to watch for this preacher."

"Think we'll get him?"

"I don't know. Chances are he won't be working the same place tomorrow. I tell you, Bert, I think there's an upswing in confidence men these days, you know it?"

"I thought they were dying out."

"For a while, yeah. But, all of a sudden, all the old confidence games are reappearing. Games that have beards on them they're so old. All of a sudden, they start cropping up." Brown shook his head. "I don't know."

"Well, they're not too serious," Kling said.

"Crime is serious," Brown said flatly.

"Oh sure," Kling said. "I just meant…Well, aside from a few bucks lost, there's never any *real* harm done."

The girl in the River Harb had had some real harm done to her.

She floated up onto the rocks near the Hamilton Bridge, and three young kids didn't know what she was at first, and then they realized, and they ran like hell for the nearest cop.

The girl was still on the rocks when the cop arrived. The cop did not like to look at dead bodies, especially dead bodies that had been in the water for any amount of time. Bloated and immense, the girl hardly looked like a girl at all. Her head hair had been completely washed away. Her body was decomposed, and fibrous strands of flesh clung to her brassiere, which, snapped by the expanding gasses in the body, miraculously clung to her though the rest of her clothing was gone. Her lower front teeth were gone, too.

The patrolman managed to keep down the bilious feeling that suddenly attacked his stomach. He went to the nearest call box and phoned in to the 87th Precinct, which house he happened to work for.

Sullivan, the sergeant who was manning the desk, said, "87th Precinct, good morning."

"This is Di Angelo," the patrolman said.

"Yeah?"

"I've got a floater near the bridge."

He gave Sullivan all the details, and then he went back to stand alongside the dead girl on the rocks, which were washed with April sunshine.

Detective Steve Carella was glad the sun was shining.

It was not that Carella didn't like rain. After all, the farmers sure needed it. And, though it may sound a bit poetic, walking hatless in the spring rain had been one of Carella's favorite pastimes before the day of his idiocy.

The day of his idiocy had been Friday, December 22.

He would never think of it without referring to it as "the day of his idiocy" because that was the day he'd allowed a young punk pusher to take his service revolver away from him and fire three shots into his chest. That had been a fine Christmas, all right. That had been a Christmas when Carella could almost hear the angels, so imbued was he with the season's spirit. That had been a Christmas when he thought he wouldn't quite make it, when he thought sure he was a goner. And then, somehow, the clouds had blown away. And where there was a painful mist before, there was a slow clearing and Teddy's face in that clearing, streaked with tears. He had recognized his wife, Teddy, first, and then slowly the rest of the hospital room had come into focus. She had leaned over the bed and rested her cheek against his, and he could feel her tears hot on his face, and he whispered hoarsely, "Cancel the wreath," in an attempt at wit that was unfunny. She had clung to him fiercely, wordlessly—wordlessly because Teddy could neither speak nor hear. She had clung to him, and then she had kissed his unfunny humor off his mouth, and then she had covered his face with kisses, holding his hand all the while, careful not to lean on his bandaged, wounded chest.

He had healed. Time heals all wounds, the wise men say.

Of course, the wise men didn't know about rain and bullet holes. When it rained, Carella's healed wounds ached. He always thought that was a bunch of bull, wounds aching when it rained. Well, it was not a bunch of bull. His wounds ached when it rained, and so he was glad the rain had stopped and the sun was shining.

The sun was shining on what had once been a girl, and Carella looked down at the travesty death had wrought, and there was momentary pain in his eyes and momentary anger, and both passed.

To Di Angelo, he said, "You find the body, Fred?"

"Some kids," Di Angelo said. "They come running to me. Jesus, it's a mess, ain't it?"

"It almost always is," Carella said. He looked at the body again, and then because certain police formalities had to be followed whenever an unknown body turned up, he took a small black pad from his back pocket. He opened the pad, slid the pencil out from under its leather loop, and wrote:

1) *Place where body found:* Washed ashore on rock pile in River Harb.
2) *Time when found:*

He looked up at Di Angelo. "When did you get here, Fred?"

Di Angelo looked at his watch. "I'd say around one-fifteen, Steve. I was just a little bit off Silvermine, and I'm generally there around…"

"One-fifteen it is," Carella said, and he wrote down the information. He then wrote, *3) Cause of death?* and *4) Time when death occurred?* and left both those items to be filled in by the ME or the coroner.

He next wrote:

5) Supposed age: 25–35.
6) Supposed profession: ?
7) Description of body:
  a) Sex: Female.
  b) Color: White.
  c) Nationality: ?
  d) Height: ?
  e) Weight: ?

There were a lot of question marks.

There were also a good many other items Carella could have listed under a description of the body. Items like build and complexion and hair and eyes and eyebrows and nose and chin and face and neck and lips and mouth and many more. And to these he could have given answers ranging from short and stocky to stout and square-shouldered, or small and pug, or square and dimpled, or thick and puffy, or any one of a hundred combinations for each category.

The trouble was that the body was a floater and pretty badly decomposed. Where an unknown body would automatically have called for a description of the eyes, the color, the shape, etc., Carella could give no such description here because the eyes had already decomposed. Where he would have liked to list the color of the girl's hair, that hair had been washed away, and he settled for a brief note: *Head hair gone. Pubic hair, blonde.* He terminated his description of the body with the boldly printed word FLOATER. That, for anyone in the know, summed up the story. Then he went on to the next item:

> *8)* *Description of clothing:* Single article of clothing is brassiere. Have lab check for laundry and dry-cleaning marks.
> *9)* *Jewelry and other objects on person:* None.

Carella closed the notebook.

"What do you make of it?" Di Angelo asked.

"You want statistics or guesses?" Carella said.

"Gee, I don't know. I was just asking."

"Well, by statistics, this girl shouldn't be dead," Carella said. "It's all a mistake."

"How so?"

"From the looks of her, I'd say she's been in the water maybe three, four months. Somebody probably reported her missing during that time—assuming she's got family or friends—so that makes her technically a missing person."

"Yeah?" Di Angelo asked, impressed as always by Carella. Di Angelo respected Carella a great deal. Part of this respect was due to the fact that they were both of Italian descent, and there was something immensely gratifying—to Di Angelo's way of thinking—about an Italian boy making good. Di Angelo felt about Carella much the same way he felt about Frank Sinatra. But the major part of Di Angelo's respect came from a thorough appreciation of the fact that Carella was a smart cop, a well-informed cop, and, on occasion, a tough cop. This, in Di Angelo's book, was a tough combination to beat.

"So let's look at the missing persons statistics," Carella said. "We've got a girl here. Well, there are usually twenty-five percent more males than females among missing persons."

"Yeah?" Di Angelo said.

"Two: She's probably somewhere between twenty-five and thirty years old. The peak age for missing persons is fifteen."

"Yeah?" DiAngelo said.

"Three: This is April. The peak month for missing persons is May, and the second peak month is September."

"How you like that?" Di Angelo said.

"So, statistically, this is all wrong." Carella sighed, and again, there was a passing film of pain in his eyes. "That doesn't make her any less dead, though," he said.

"No," Di Angelo said, shaking his head.

"One guess of a semi-technical nature," Carella said. "Five'll get you ten she's an out-of-towner."

Di Angelo nodded and then glanced up to the highway where two police sedans had pulled up. "Here's the lab boys and the photographers," he said, and then, as if he were certain such would not be the case now that they were on the scene, he looked down at the dead girl and said, "Rest in peace."

If Carella's interest in the floater, at this stage of the game, was a more or less fleeting one, there were those involved in police work who gave the decomposed body and its single article of clothing a much closer and more thorough inspection.

The girl's brassiere was sent to the police laboratory. The girl's body was sent to the morgue.

Sam Grossman was a police lieutenant and also a skilled laboratory technician. He was a big man with a rough-hewn face and big hands. He wore glasses because his eyes were not too good. There was a gentility about him that belied the fact that he dealt with cold scientific facts and often with the facts of death. He ran a clean laboratory, and his men got results. His laboratory was divided into seven sections, and it covered a good deal of the first floor of the Headquarters building on High Street downtown. The seven sections were:

1) Chemical and physical.
2) Biological.
3) General.
4) Firearms.
5) Questioned documents.
6) Photographic.
7) Mechanical.

The brassiere was turned over to the physical section first. The gentlemen who examined it there paid little or no attention to the fact that this single item of clothing is responsible for one of the most widespread and nationally advertised fetishes in America. They didn't care whether or not the secret was in the circle, or whether or not anyone had dreamt she was a ballerina in this particular brassiere, or whether or not there was any hidden treasure to be found. They were interested in the undergarment as it applied to one thing, and one thing alone—the identity of the dead girl.

Most articles of clothing, you see, will carry either laundry or dry-cleaning marks. Sam Grossman was proud of the fact that his lab had the most comprehensive file of laundry marks in the nation. In a matter of minutes, provided there was a mark in the article of clothing, Sam's men could pinpoint the exact laundry that had stamped the mark.

The brassiere carried no visible laundry marks. It would have been simpler if it had. It's always simpler when you can see something with the naked eye. In truth, though, it wasn't very much more difficult to put the brassiere on the long white counter over which hung the ultraviolet lights. A flip of the switch, and the counter turned a lovely shade of purple, and the brassiere turned a lovely shade of purple, and Sam's men turned it over and over, searching for the luminous Phantom Fast laundry mark that many laundries use. The Phantom Fast mark is a good idea since it leaves no unsightly numbers on the back of your shirt collar or the seat of your underpants. It means compiling a separate set of marks for police files, but think of how pretty your shirts look. The only thing that'll bring out a Phantom Fast mark is ultraviolet light, and hell, police labs are crawling with that kind of light.

The only trouble with the dead girl's brassiere was that it didn't carry a Phantom Fast mark, either.

Faced with the fact that the girl probably did her own laundry, but otherwise unfazed, Sam's men began putting the bra through a series of chemical tests to determine whether or not it held any peculiar stains.

Meanwhile, back at the morgue...

The assistant medical examiner was a man named Paul Blaney. He had been examining dead bodies for a good many years, but he still could not get used to floaters. He had been examining this particular dead body for nigh onto two hours, and he still could not get used to floaters. He had estimated that the dead girl was approximately thirty-five years of age, that her weight while she was alive (according to her five-foot-three-and-a-half-inch height and her large bone structure) was probably somewhere around 125 pounds, and that her head hair (judging from the color of her pubic hair) was probably blonde.

Her lower front teeth had been lost in the water, and her upper front teeth were in good condition, although her upper back teeth and her lower back teeth had a good many fillings and a good many cavities. The upper right second molar had been extracted a long time ago and never replaced. Blaney had prepared a dental chart to be compared with the dental chart of any suspected missing person.

He had also made a methodical scrutiny of the girl's body for identifying marks or scars and had concluded that she'd once had an appendectomy (there was a long scar across her belly), that she'd been vaccinated on her left thigh rather than on either of her arms, that there was a duster of birthmarks at the base of her spinal column, and unusual in a woman, that there was a small tattoo on the fold of skin between her right thumb and forefinger. The tattoo was a simple heart, the point of which ran toward the arm. There was a single word within the heart. The tattoo looked like this:

Blaney estimated that the body had been submerged for at least three to four months. The epidermis of both hands was lost, and he sighed a forlorn sigh for his brothers of toil in the police laboratory because he knew this would mean extra work for them. And then, with a great show of distaste and a maximum of somehow remarkably detached efficiency, he cut off the fingers and thumb of each hand and wrapped them up for delivery to Sam Grossman.

Then he began working on the dead girl's heart.

It requires a certain amount of dispassionate, emotionless patience to lift fingerprint impressions from fingers and thumbs that have been cut from a cadaver.

If the dead girl had been in the water for a comparatively short period of time, Sam Grossman's men could have dried off each finger with a soft towel and then—in order to smooth out the so-called washerwoman's skin effect—have injected glycerin beneath the fingertip skin. They could then have taken their prints with ease.

Unfortunately, the girl had not been in the water for a short period of time.

Nor had she been in the water only long enough to wear away the friction ridges of her fingers. Had this been the case, the lab boys would have cut away the skin of each fingertip, placing these snips in separate test tubes with formaldehyde solution. Assuming the papillary ridges were intact on the outer surface of the skin, one of Sam's men would have put on a rubber glove, placed the piece of skin on his index finger, and then rolled finger, glove, and skin on an inking plate—as if the piece of skin were actually his own finger—and then recorded it on the fingerprint form.

Even if the papillary ridges had been destroyed, the papillary pattern would be found on the inner surface of the skin, and a good photograph could be had if the skin were attached to a piece of cardboard, inner surface out, and the picture taken in oblique light.

Unfortunately, the unidentified dead girl had been in the water for close to four months, and the laboratory technicians had to turn to more tedious and inventive methods of getting their fingerprints.

In the hands of less-skilled operators than Sam Grossman's men, an attempt at the papillary method may have proved less expedient and less fruitful. But Sam's men were whizzes, and so they took each finger and each thumb, and they stood over Bunsen burners and slowly, methodically, doggedly dried the fingers, passing them over the flame, their hands moving in short arcs, back and forth, back and forth, until each finger had shrunk and dried.

Then, at last, they were able to touch each finger lightly with printer's ink and take their impressions.

Their impressions did not tell them who the dead girl was.

One copy of her prints was sent to the Bureau of Criminal Identification.

One copy was sent to the FBI.

A third copy was sent to the Bureau of Missing Persons.

A fourth was sent to Homicide North—since all suicides or suspected suicides are treated exactly like homicides.

And, finally, a copy was sent to the Detective Division of the 87th Precinct, in which territory the body had been found.

Sam Grossman's men washed their hands.

There was something about Paul Blaney that made Carella's flesh crawl. Perhaps it was the idea of Blaney dealing with death as an occupation, but Carella suspected it was the man's personality and not his job. He had, after all, dealt with many men whose occupation was death. With Blaney, however, it seemed to be more a preoccupation than an occupation, and so Carella stood before him, towering over him, and he could feel a nest of spiders in his stomach, and he wanted to scratch himself or take a bath.

The two men stood in the clean antiseptic examination room of the morgue alongside the stainless steel table, with its troughs to gather in the flow of blood, with its stainless steel basin to capture the blood and hold it in a ruby pool. Blaney was a short man with a balding head and a scraggly black mustache. He was the only man Carella had ever met who owned violet eyes.

Carella stood opposite him, a big man, but not a heavy one. He gave an impression of athletic tightness; every muscle and sinew in his body pulled into a wiry bundle of power. His eyes were brown, slanting downward to meet high cheekbones so that his face had an almost Oriental look. He wore his brown hair short. He wore a gray sports jacket and charcoal slacks, and the jacket stretched wide across the breadth of his shoulders, angled in sharply to cover narrow hips and a flat, hard stomach.

"What do you make of it?" he asked Blaney.

"I hate floaters," Blaney said. "I hate to look at them. The goddamned things make me sick."

"Nobody likes floaters," Carella said.

"Me especially," Blaney said, nodding vigorously. "They always give me the floaters. If you've got seniority around here, you can pull anything you want. So I'm low man on the totem pole. So whenever a goddamned floater comes in, everybody else suddenly has corpses in Siberia. Is that fair? That I should get the floaters?"

"Somebody's got to get them."

"Sure, but why me? Listen, I don't complain about anything they give me. We've had stiffs in here so burned up you wouldn't even know they were human. You ever handle charred flesh? Okay, but do I complain? We get automobile accident victims where a guy's head is hanging from his neck by one strand of skin. I take it in stride. I'm an ME, and you've got to take the good ones with the bad ones. But why should I get all the floaters? How come nobody else gets the floaters?"

"Look—" Carella started, but Blaney was just gathering steam, just picking up speed.

"There isn't anybody in the goddamn department who does a better job than me. Trouble is, I haven't got seniority. It's all politics. Who do you think gets the nice posh jobs? The old fuddies who've been cutting up stiffs for forty years. But I do a neat, thorough job. Thorough. I'm thorough. I don't overlook anything. Not a thing. So I get the floaters!"

"Maybe they figure you're so expert they wouldn't trust them to anyone else," Carella said drily.

"Huh?" Blaney said. "Expert?"

"Certainly. You're a good man, Blaney. Floaters are tough. You can't trust them with just any damn butcher."

Blaney's violet eyes softened a shade. "I never thought of it that way," he said. He smiled slightly, and then the smile vanished before a suspicious lowering of his brows as he thought the problem over again.

"What about this one?" Carella asked, not wanting Blaney to start thinking too hard.

"Oh," Blaney said. "Yeah. Well, I got a report there—all the junk. Been in the water about four months, I would say. I just got done with the heart."

"And?"

"You know anything about the heart?"

"Not very much, no."

"Right and left chambers, you see. Blood passes through, gets pumped around the body...Oh hell, I can't give a layman an anatomy lesson."

"I didn't ask for one," Carella said.

"Anyway, I did the Gettler test. Idea is that if someone drowns, water passes from the lungs into the blood. We can tell pretty well this way whether a person drowned in fresh water or salt water."

"How so?"

"If it was fresh water, the blood in the left side of the heart will have a lower-than-normal chloride content. Salt water, the blood in the left side of the heart will have a higher-than-normal amount of chloride."

"This girl was found in the River Harb," Carella said. "That's fresh water, isn't it?"

"Sure. But according to Smith—you know, Smith, Glaister, and Von Neureiter..."

"Go ahead," Carella said.

"According to Smith, if a person is already dead when he's thrown into the water, it's impossible for any water to get into that person's left heart." Blaney paused. "In other words, if we find no water in the left heart during autopsy, we can safely assume that person didn't drown. That person was dead before he hit the water."

"Yes?" Carella said, interested now.

"This little girl didn't have a drop of water there, Carella. This little girl didn't drown."

Carella stared deep into Blaney's violet eyes. "How'd she die?" he asked.

"Acute arsenic poisoning," Blaney said. "Greatest amount of it was found in the stomach and intestines. Indicates oral ingestion. The whole system was not impregnated, so we can chalk off chronic poisoning. This was acute. She may, in fact, have died just a few hours after she swallowed the stuff."

Blaney scratched the top of his balding head.

"In fact," he added, "you may even have yourself a homicide here."

Life, if you take a somewhat dim and cynical view of it, is something like a big con game.

Look around you, friends, and see the confidence men.

"I have in my hand right here, ladies and gentlemen, a bar of So-Soap. This is the only soap on the market that contains neocenephrotaneticin, which we call Neo No. 7. Neo No. 7 puts an invisible film of visible filmy acentodoids on the epidermal glottifram..."

"If I am elected, friends, I can promise you good clean government. And why can I promise you good abusive government? Because I am sincere and untrustworthy. I am honest and selfishly domineering. I am the biggest, the most attentive, the most fastidious violator of the Mann Act, and I can promise..."

"Look, George, where else can you get a deal like this one? We are willing to construct the whole damned thing, take full responsibility for the job, and all it'll cost you is around two million dollars. And, with that, you get my own personal guarantee. My own personal guarantee."

"Baby, what I'm trying to tell you is I never felt like this before. I mean, when you walk into a room, Jesus, the room lights up. Do you know what I mean? My heart begins to go up and down like a yo-yo. There's a light that comes from you, baby, a light that fills up the sky. If that ain't love, I don't know what love is. Believe me, baby, I never felt like this. Like walking on air with my head in the clouds, like wanting to sing all the time. I love you, sweetheart. I love you like crazy. So why don't you be a good girl and take off that dress, huh?"

"I'll be honest with you. That car had seventy-five thousand miles on it before we turned back the speedometer. Also, that's a new paint job. We don't trust new paint jobs. Who knows what's under that paint, friend. I wouldn't sell you that dog if you begged me. But step over here a minute and take a look at this lavender-and-red convertible that was owned by the maiden aunt of a Protestant minister who used it only once a week to do her marketing around the corner. Now, this car…"

NOW

FOR THE FIRST TIME IN PUBLISHING HISTORY

We are proud to announce the most compelling novel since *Gone With The Wind.*

THE TATTERED PICCOLO

A Book of the Month Club selection…

A Literary Guild selection…

A Reader's Digest Book Club selection…

Purchased by a major movie company as a vehicle for Tab Hunter…

6,000,000 copies now in print!

Rush to your bookseller. He may still have a few in stock!

"The trouble with this guy's parties is he doesn't know how to mix martinis. It takes a certain amount of finesse, you know. Now, here's my formula. You take a water glass full of gin..."

"Hello, friends, I'm George Grosnick. This is my brother Louie Grosnick. We make Grosnick Beer...All right, Louie, you tell them..."

It's the hard sell and the soft sell, anywhere you go, everywhere you go. It comes at you a hundred times a day, and maybe it's stretching a point to say that every human being has his own confidence game, that every human being has a tiny touch of larceny in his soul, but be careful, friend; the television is on, and that man is pointing at *you*!

The man in the dark-blue suit was a con man.

He sat in the hotel lobby waiting for a man named Jamison. He had first seen Jamison at the railroad station when the train from Boston pulled in. He had followed Jamison to the hotel, and now he sat in the lobby and waited for him to appear because the man in the dark-blue suit had plans for Jamison.

He was a good-looking man, tall, with even features and a friendly mouth and eyes. He dressed immaculately. His white shirt was spotless, and his suit was freshly pressed. His black shoes were highly polished, and amazing in this elastic-top-socked age, his socks were held firmly in place with garters.

He was holding a guidebook to the city in his hand.

He looked at his watch. It was close to 6:30, and Jamison should be down soon if he planned on having dinner at all. The lobby bustled with activity. A beer company was holding eliminations for its yearly glamour girl contest, and models swarmed over the thick rugs, accompanied by press agents and photographers.

All of the models looked the same. The hair-coloring varied, but otherwise, they all looked the same. They were, in essence, symbols created by con men. They were, too, in essence, con men themselves.

He saw Jamison come out of one of the elevators. Quickly, he rose and stood with the guidebook open at the top of the steps leading to the street. He could see Jamison, from the corner of his eye, moving toward the steps. He buried himself in the guidebook, and when Jamison was abreast of him, he moved sharply to the left, colliding with him.

Jamison looked startled. He was a stout man with a red face, dressed in a brown pinstripe. The con man fumbled for the fallen guidebook, and then, from his knees, said, "Gosh, I'm sorry. Excuse me, please."

"That's all right," Jamison said.

The con man stood up. "I got so involved in this book I guess I wasn't watching where I...Say, you're all right, aren't you?"

"Yes, I'm fine," Jamison said.

"Well, I'm certainly glad to hear that. This darn book is Greek to me. I can tell you that I'm from Boston, you see. I've been trying to make out the street—"

"Boston?" Jamison said, interested. "Really?"

"Well, not exactly. A suburb. West Newton. Do you know it?"

"Why, sure I do," Jamison said. "I've lived in Boston all my life."

The con man's face opened with delighted surprise. "Is that right? Well, I'll be...Say, how do you like that?"

"Small world, ain't it?" Jamison said, grinning.

"Listen, this calls for something," the con man said. "I'm superstitious that way. Something like this happens, it calls for something. Let me buy you a drink."

"Well, I was just on my way to dinner," Jamison said.

"Fine, we'll have a drink together, and then you can go on your way. Tell you the truth, I'm tickled I ran into you. I don't know a soul in this town."

"I suppose we could have a drink," Jamison said. "You here on business?"

"Yes," the con man said. "Marlboro Tractor Corporation—know them?"

"No. I'm in textiles myself," Jamison said.

"Well, no matter. Shall we try the hotel bar, or do you want to scout up something else? Hotel bars are a little stiff, don't you think?" He had already taken Jamison's arm and was leading him down the steps.

"Well, I never really—"

"Sure. Seemed to me there were a lot of bars on the next street. Why don't we try one of them?" He passed Jamison through the revolving doors, and when they reached the sidewalk, he looked up at the buildings, seemingly bewildered. "Now, let me see," he said. "Which is east and which is west?"

"That's east," Jamison said, pointing.

"Fine."

The con man introduced himself as Charlie Parsons. Jamison said his first name was Elliot. Together, they walked up the street, looking at the various bars, deciding against one or another for various reasons—most of which Parsons offered.

When they came to a place called The Red Cockatoo, Parsons took Jamison's arm and said, "Now, this looks like a nice place. How about it?"

"Suits me fine," Jamison said. "One bar's just about as good as another, the way I look at it."

They were heading for the entrance door when the door opened and a man in a gray suit stepped out onto the sidewalk.

He was a pleasant-looking man in his late thirties, a shock of red hair topping his head. He seemed very much in a hurry.

"Say," Parsons said, "excuse me a minute."

The redheaded man stopped. "Yes?" he said. He still seemed in a hurry.

"What kind of a place is this?" Parsons asked.

"Huh?"

"The bar. You just came out of it. Is it a nice place?"

"Oh," the redheaded man said. "The bar. Tell you the truth, I don't know. I just stopped in there to make a phone call."

"Oh, I see," Parsons said. "Well, thank you," and he turned away from the redheaded man, seemingly to enter the bar with Jamison.

"It's the damnedest thing, ain't it?" the redhead said. "I haven't been in this city for close to five years. So I come in on a trip, and I've been calling old friends since the minute I arrived, and all of them are busy tonight."

Parsons turned, smiling. "Oh?" he said. "Where you from?"

"Wilmington," the redhead said.

"We're out-of-towners, too," Parsons explained. "Listen, if you haven't anything else to do, why don't you join us for a drink?"

"Well, gee, that's awfully kind of you," the redhead said. "But I wouldn't want to impose."

"No imposition at all," Parsons said. He turned to Jamison. "You don't mind, do you, Elliot?"

"Not at all," Jamison said. "More the merrier."

"Well, in that case, I'd enjoy it a lot," the redhead said.

"I'm Charlie Parsons," Parsons said, "and this is Elliot Jamison."

"Pleased to know you," the redhead said. "I'm Frank O'Neill."

The men shook hands all around.

"Well, let's get those drinks," Parsons said, and they went into the bar. They took a table in the corner, and after they'd made themselves comfortable, Parsons said, "Are you here on business, Frank?"

"No, no," O'Neill said. "Pleasure. Strictly pleasure. Some stock I've been holding took a big jump, and I decided to take those extra dividends and have myself a hell of a time." He leaned over the table, and his voice lowered. "I've got more than three thousand dollars with me. I think I'll be able to have a whopper with that, eh?" He burst out laughing, and Parsons and Jamison laughed with him, and then they ordered a round of drinks.

"Drink whatever you like and as much as you like," O'Neill said, "because this is all on me."

"Oh, no," Parsons said. "We invited you to join us."

"I don't care," O'Neill insisted. "If it wasn't for you fellows, I'd be on the town alone. Hell, that's no fun."

"Well," Jamison said, "I really don't think it's fair for you—"

"It certainly wouldn't be fair, Elliot. We'll each pay for a round, how's that?"

"No, sir!" O'Neill objected. He seemed to be a pretty hot-tempered fellow, and somehow, this business of who should pay for the drinks was upsetting him. He raised his voice and said, "I'm paying for everything. I've got three thousand dollars, and if that's not enough to pay for a few lousy drinks, I'd like to know what is."

"That's not the point, Frank," Parsons said. "Really. You'd embarrass me."

"Me, too," Jamison said. "I think Charlie's right. We'll each pay for a round."

"I'll tell you what I'll do," O'Neal said. "I'll match you for the drinks. How's that?"

"Match us?" Parsons said. "What do you mean?"

"We'll match coins. Here." He reached into his pocket and pulled out a quarter. The drinks had come by this time, and the men sipped a little from their glasses. Parsons took a quarter from his pocket, and then Jamison took a quarter from his.

"Here's the way we'll work it," O'Neill said. "We'll all flip together. Odd man, the fellow who has a head when the other two have tails—or tails when the other two have heads—doesn't pay. Then the other two flip to see who does pay. Okay?"

"Fair enough," Parsons said.

"Okay, here we go," O'Neill said. The three men flipped their coins and covered them. When they uncovered, Parsons and O'Neill were showing heads. Jamison was showing tails.

"Well, you're out of it," O'Neill said. "It's between you and me now, Charlie."

They flipped.

"How do we work this?" Parsons asked.

"You have to say whether we match or don't match," O'Neill said.

"I say we match."

They uncovered the coins. Both men were showing tails.

"You lose," Parsons said.

"I always do," O'Neill said, and somehow—in spite of his earlier eagerness to pay for the drinks—he seemed miffed now that he actually *had* to pay for them. "I'm just plain unlucky," he said. "Some fellows go to carnivals, throw a few baseballs at a stuffed monkey, come home winning a power lawn mower. They buy one ticket in a raffle, and they win the new Dodge convertible. Me, I buy six books of tickets, I get nothing. I ain't never won anything in my whole life. I'm an unlucky son of a gun, all right."

"Well," Parsons said in a seeming attempt to cajole O'Neill, "I'll pay for the next round."

"Oh, no," O'Neill said. "We'll match for the next round."

"We haven't even finished this round," Jamison said politely.

"Makes no never mind," O'Neill said. "I'm gonna lose, anyway. Come on, let's match."

"You shouldn't take that attitude," Parsons said. "I believe that, in matching, or in cards, or in things like that, you can control your own luck. No, really, you can. It's all in the mind. If you go into this thinking you're going to lose, why, you *will* lose."

"I'll lose no matter what," O'Neill said. "Come on, let's match."

The men flipped their coins.

Parsons showed heads.

O'Neill showed heads.

Jamison showed tails.

"You're a real lucky fink," O'Neill said, his irritation mounting. "You could jump into a tub of horseshit and come out smelling of lavender."

"Well, I'm not usually lucky," Jamison said apologetically. He exchanged a quick glance with Parsons, whose uplifted eyebrows clearly expressed the opinion that O'Neill was a strange duck, indeed.

"Come on, come on," O'Neill said, "let's get this over with. This time I'll call." He and Parsons flipped their coins and covered them. "We match," O'Neill said.

Parsons uncovered heads.

O'Neill uncovered tails and said, "Son of a bitch! You see? I never win, never! Goddammit, let's match for the next round."

"We're already a round ahead of ourselves," Parsons said gently.

"You want me to pay for all the damn drinks, is that it?" O'Neill shouted.

"Well, no, no, that's not it."

"Why won't you give me a chance to win back what I've lost?"

Parsons smiled gently and looked to Jamison for assistance.

Jamison cleared his throat. "You misunderstand, Frank," he said genially. "We hadn't planned on making this a big drinking night. As a matter of fact, I haven't even had dinner yet."

"Is three rounds of drinks a big drinking night?" O'Neill asked irritably. "I say we match for the third round. I *insist* we match for the third round."

Parsons smiled weakly. "Frank, it's really academic. We may not even get to the third round. Look, let me pay for the last two rounds, huh? This party was my idea, and I'm a little embarrassed—"

"I lost, and I'll pay!" O'Neill said firmly. "Now, come on, let's match for the third round."

Parsons sighed. Jamison shrugged and caught Parsons's eye. The men flipped their coins.

"Heads," Jamison said.

"Tails," Parsons said.

"Tails," O'Neill said sourly. "This Jamison never loses, does he? By God, he never loses. Come on, it's between you and me, Charlie."

"It's my turn to call, isn't it?" Parsons asked.

"Yes, yes," O'Neill said impatiently. "It's your goddamn turn to call." He flipped and covered his coin.

Parsons flipped, covered the coin, and said, "We won't match this time." He lifted his hand—tails.

O'Neill uncovered his coin. "Heads! I could have told you! I could have told you even before I looked at the damn thing. I never win! Never!" He rose angrily. "Where's the men's room? I'm going to the men's room!"

He stalked away from the table, and Parsons watched him.

"I'd like to apologize," Parsons said. "When I invited him, I had no idea he was such a sore loser."

"Hell, the matching was all his idea, anyway," Jamison said.

"God, he really got riled up, didn't he?"

"He's a peculiar fellow," Jamison said, shaking his head.

Parsons seemed to have a sudden idea. "Listen," he said, "let's have some fun with him."

"What kind of fun?"

"Well, he's a sore loser—worst I've ever seen."

"Me, too," Jamison said.

"He said he's got three thousand dollars with him. Let's take it away from him."

"What?" Jamison said, suddenly righteously indignant.

"Not for keeps. We'll take it away from him and then give it all back later."

"Take it away? But I don't understand."

"We'll change the matching rules when he comes back. We'll make it odd man *loses*. All right, we'll make sure that your coin and my coin always match. Nine times out of ten, *he'll* be odd man. And loser."

"How we going to do that?" Jamison asked, beginning to get interested in the idea of a little sport.

"Simple. Keep your coin on end so you can shove it down to either heads or tails. If I touch my nose with my finger, make your coin show heads. If I don't touch it, show tails."

"I see," Jamison said, grinning.

"We'll keep raising the stakes. We'll clean him out, and then we'll give him back his money. Okay?"

Jamison couldn't keep the grin off his face. "Boy," he said, "he's really going to blow his stack."

"Until he knows it's all a gag," Parsons said. He patted Jamison on the back. "Here he comes. Now, let me handle this."

"All right," Jamison said, secretly beginning to enjoy himself.

O'Neill came back to the table and sat. He seemed angry as hell. "The second round come yet?" he asked.

"No," Parsons said. "You know, Frank, it's your attitude that makes you lose. I was just telling that to Elliot here."

"Attitude, my ass," O'Neill said. "I'm just unlucky."

"I can prove it to you," Parsons said. "Come on, let's match a little more."

"I thought you said this wasn't going to be a drinking night," O'Neill said suspiciously.

"We'll match for a few bucks, all right?"

"I'll lose," O'Neill said.

"Why not give Charlie's theory a chance?" Jamison put in.

"Sure," Parsons said. "I've got a little money with me. Let's see how fast you can take it away from me, using my theory." He paused, then turned to Jamison. "You've got some money with you, haven't you, Elliot?"

"About two hundred and fifty dollars," Jamison said. "I don't like to carry too much with me. You never know."

"That's wise," Parsons said, nodding. "What do you say, Frank?"

"All right, all right, what's your theory?"

"Just concentrate on winning, that's all. Think with all your might. Just think, *I'm going to win, I'm going to win*, that's all."

"It won't work, but I'm game. How much do we bet?"

"Let's start with five," Parsons said. "To make it quicker, we'll do it this way. Odd man loses. He pays each of the other players five bucks. How does that sound?"

"Well, that sounds a little stee—" Jamison started.

"That sounds fine to me," O'Neill said. Parsons winked at Jamison.

Jamison gave a slight nod of acknowledgement and then hastily said, "Yes, that sounds fine to me, too."

They began matching.

With remarkable regularity, O'Neill kept losing. Then, perhaps because Parsons wanted to make it look good, Jamison began to lose a little, too. The men matched silently. Their table was in a corner of the place, protected from sight by a translucent glass wall. It is doubtful, anyway, that anyone would have stopped the men from their innocent coin-matching. They flipped, uncovered, and exchanged bills. In a short while, O'Neill had lost something like $400. Jamison had lost close to $200. Parsons winked at Jamison every now and then, just to let him know that everything was proceeding according to plan. O'Neill kept complaining to Jamison—who was losing along with him—about Parsons's theory. "The only one that goddamn theory works for is him himself," O'Neill said.

They kept matching.

Jamison did not lose as much now. O'Neill kept losing, and he got angrier with each flip of the coin. Finally, he looked at both men and said, "Say, what is this?"

"What's what?" Parsons asked.

"I've dropped nearly six hundred dollars so far." He turned to Jamison. "How much have you lost?"

Jamison did a little mental calculation. "Oh, about two hundred thirty-five, something like that."

"And you?" O'Neill said to Parsons.

"I'm winning," Parsons said.

O'Neill looked at his two companions with a long, steady gaze. "You wouldn't be trying to fleece me by any chance, would you?" he asked.

"Fleece?" Parsons asked.

"You wouldn't be a pair of swindlers by any chance, would you?" O'Neill asked.

Jamison could hardly keep the grin off his face. Parsons winked at him.

"What makes you say that?" Parsons asked.

O'Neill rose suddenly. "I'm calling a cop," he said.

The grin dropped from Jamison's face. "Hey, now," he said, "wait a minute. We were just—"

Parsons, sitting secure with Jamison's $235 and O'Neill's $600 in his pocket, said, "No need to get sore, Frank. A game's a game."

"Besides," Jamison said, "we were only—"

Parsons put an arm on his sleeve and winked at him. "The breaks are the breaks, Frank," he said to O'Neill.

"And crooks are crooks," O'Neill said. "I'm getting a cop." He started away from the table.

Jamison's face went white. "Charlie," he said, "we've got to stop him. A joke is a joke, but Jesus—"

"I'll get him," Parsons said, rising. He chuckled. "God, he's a weird duck, isn't he? I'll bring him right back. You wait here."

O'Neill had already reached the door. As he stepped outside, Parsons called, "Hey, Frank! Wait a minute!" and ran out after him.

Jamison sat at the table alone, still frightened, telling himself he would never again be party to a practical joke.

It wasn't until a half hour later that he realized the joke was on him.

He told himself it couldn't be.

Then he sat for another half hour.

Then he went to the nearest police station and told a detective named Arthur Brown the story.

Brown listened patiently and then took a description of the two professional coin-matchers who had conned Jamison out of $235.

P. T. Barnum rolled over in his grave, chuckling.

The Missing Persons Bureau is a part of the Detective Division, and so the two men Bert Kling talked to were detectives.

One was called Ambrose.

The other was called Bartholdi.

"Naturally," Bartholdi said, "we got nothing to do here but concern ourselves with floaters."

"Naturally," Ambrose said.

"We only got reports on sixteen missing kids under the age of ten today, but we got nothing to do but worry about a stiff been in the water for six months."

"Four months," Kling corrected.

"Pardon me," Bartholdi said.

"With dicks from the 87th," Ambrose said, "you got to be careful. You slip up by a couple of months, they jump down your throat. They got very technical flatfoots at the 87th."

"We try our hardest," Kling said drily.

"Humanitarians all," Bartholdi said. "They worry about floaters. They got concern for the human race."

"Us," Ambrose said, "all we got to worry about is the three-year-old kids who vanish from their front stoops. That's all we got to worry about."

"You'd think I was asking to spend the night with your sister," Kling said. "All I want is a look at your files."

"I'd rather you spent the night with my sister," Bartholdi said. "You might be disappointed since she's only eight years old, but I'd still rather."

"It ain't that we don't believe in interdepartmental cooperation," Ambrose said. "There ain't nothing we like better than helping out fellow flatfoots. Ain't that a fact, Romeo?"

Romeo Bartholdi nodded. "Tell him about our war record, Mike."

Ambrose said, "It was us who went to the Pacific after World War II to help clear up all that unidentified dead problem."

"If you cleaned up the whole Pacific Theater," Kling said, "you should be able to help me with one floater."

"The trouble with flatfoots," Bartholdi said, "is they got no heads for clerical work. We've got a dandy filing system here, you see? If we let dicks from all over the city come in and foul it up, we'd never be able to identify *anybody* anymore."

"Well, I'm glad you've got such a real nice filing system," Kling said. "Do you plan on keeping it a secret from the rest of the department, or will you throw open the files during Open School Week?"

"Another thing I like about the bulls from the 87th," Ambrose said, "is that they are all so comical. When one of them is around, you can hardly keep from wetting your pants."

"With glee," Bartholdi said.

"That's what makes a good cop," Ambrose expanded. "Humor, humaneness, and devotion to detail."

"Plus, the patience of Job," Kling said. "Do I get a peek at the goddamn files, or don't I?"

"Temper, temper," Bartholdi said.

"How far back do you want to go?" Ambrose asked.

"About six months."

"I thought she was in the water for only four?"

"She may have been reported missing before then."

"Clever, clever," Bartholdi said. "God, this city would fall to smoldering ashes were it not for the 87th Precinct."

"All right, screw you," Kling said, turning. "I'll tell the lieutenant your files aren't open for our inspection. So long, fellers."

"He's running home to mama," Bartholdi said, unfazed.

"Mama's liable to be upset," Kling said. "Mama doesn't mind a good joke, but not on the city's time."

"All work and no play…" Bartholdi started and then cut himself short when he saw that Kling actually was leaving. "All right, sorehead," he said, "come look at the files. Come drown in the files. We've got enough missing persons here to keep you going for a year."

"Thanks a lot," Kling said, and he followed the detectives down the corridor.

"We try to keep them cross-indexed," Ambrose said. "This ain't the IB, but we do our level best. We got 'em alphabetically, and we got 'em chronologically—according to when they were reported missing—and we got 'em broken down male and female."

"The boys with the boys, and the girls with the girls," Bartholdi said.

"There's everything you need in each of the separate folders. Medical reports where we could get 'em, dental charts, even letters and documents in some of the folders."

"Don't mix the folders up," Bartholdi said. "That would mean getting a beautiful blonde police stenographer in to straighten them out again."

"And we don't cotton to beautiful blondes around here," Ambrose said.

"We kick 'em out in the street whenever they come knocking."

"That's because we're both respectable married men."

"Who resist all temptations," Bartholdi concluded. "Here are the files." He made a grandiloquent sweeping gesture with one arm, indicating the banks and banks of green filing cabinets that lined the walls of the room. "This is April, and you want to go back six months. That'd put you in November." He made a vague gesture with one hand. "That's over there someplace." He winked at Ambrose. "Now, are we cooperating, or *are* we?"

"You're the most cooperative," Kling said.

"Hope you find what you need," Ambrose said, opening the door. "Come on, Romeo."

Bartholdi followed him out. Kling sighed, looked at the filing cabinets, and then lighted a cigarette. There was a sign on one of the walls, and the sign read: SHUFFLE THEM, JIGGLE THEM, MAUL THEM, CARESS THEM—BUT LEAVE THEM THE WAY YOU FOUND THEM!

He walked around the room until he came to the cabinet containing the file of persons who were reported missing in November of the preceding year. He opened the top drawer of the cabinet, pulled up a straight-back wooden chair upon which to prop his foot, and doggedly began leafing through the folders.

The work was not exactly unpleasant, but it was far from exciting. The average misconception of the city detective, of course, is one of a tough, big man wearing a shoulder holster facing a desperate criminal and shooting it out in the streets. Kling was big, not so tough, and he carried his service revolver in a leather holster clipped into his right back pocket. He was not shooting it out with anyone at the moment, desperate or not. The only desperation he knew was of a quiet sort, which drives many city detectives into the nearest loony bin, where they silently pick at the coverlets. Kling, at the moment, was involved in routine—and routine is the most routine thing in the world.

Routine is what makes you wash your face and shave and brush your teeth in the morning.

Routine is the business of inserting a key into the ignition switch, twisting the key, starting the car, and putting it into drive before you can go anyplace.

Routine is answering a letter with a polite thank-you and then answering the resultant thank-you letter with another letter stating, "You're welcome."

Routine is the list of questions you ask the surviving wife of an automobile accident victim.

Routine is the tag you fill out and attach to a piece of evidence.

Routine is the report you type back at the squadroom.

Routine is a deadly dull bore, and it isn't even crashing, and detectives know routine in triplicate, and the detective who isn't patient with a typewriter—no matter what his method of typing may be—doesn't last very long in the detective division.

When you've looked at missing person report after missing person report, you begin to wish you were missing yourself. After a while, they all begin to blend together into a big mass of humanity that has formed a conspiracy to bore you to death. After a while, you don't know who has the birthmark on her left breast or who has the tattoo on his big toe. After a while, you don't even care. There are amusing breaks in the routine, of course, but these are few and far between. Like the husband and wife, for example, who both vanished on the same day and who later filed missing person reports for each other. Very comical. Kling grinned, picturing the husband as an Alec Guinness type of character lolling with a brunette in Brazil. He formed no mental picture of the wife. He lighted another cigarette and continued his search for someone who might possibly resemble the 87th's floater.

He consumed two packages of cigarettes while perusing the files. He had finished the first pack before lunch. He went out for a ham sandwich and a cup of coffee, which he took back to the bureau with him, together with a fresh package of cigarettes and a warning to himself to go slow on the coffin nails. By the end of the day, he had finished the second pack, and he'd also collected a sizable pile of folders that could possibly tie in with the floater. One report looked particularly promising. Kling opened the folder again and went over the material inside it.

POLICE DEPARTMENT
REPORT OF MISSING PERSON

Det. Dist. —— Squad ——
Case No. ——
M.P. Bur. No. 72465018
Date of This Report 11/7

Surname	First Name	Initials	Nativity	Sex	Age	Color
PROSCHEK,	MARY LOUISE		U.S.A.	F	33	W

Address	Last Seen At	Date and Time Seen
1112 Main, Scranton, Pa.	Home address	10/31 11:45 ~~a.m.~~ p.m.
Probable Destination	**Cause of Absence**	**Date and Time Reported**
This city	?	11/7 8:15 a.m. ~~p.m.~~

PHYSICAL note peculiarities	CLOTHING—give color, fabric, style, label, where possible (strike out irrelevant words)		MISCELLANEOUS INFORMATION
Height: ft. 5 in. 3½	Headgear: Hatless		Occupation or School: File clerk
Weight: 128	~~Over or~~ Top Coat: Blue reversible—red inside		Ever Fingerprinted? Where & When? Never
Build: Stout	~~Suit or Dress~~: Navy blue shantung, white buttons up front		Dry Cleaner Marks: Dress and coat—X3175 Do-Brite Cleaners, Scranton
Complexion: Fair	Jacket or Sweater: None	Vest: ——	Laundry Marks: ——
Hair: Blond	Shirt or Blouse: None	Scarf: Red silk	Photo P'rnd: Yes; Prev. Missing: No
Eyes: Blue	Tie or Fur Piece: None	Gloves: Red cotton	Publicity Desired? Yes; Soc. Sec. # 119-16-4683
Glasses, Type: ——	Trousers or Skirt: ——		Preliminary Investigation
Mustache—Beard: ——	Hose: Natural nylon, seamless		Desk Officer: Sgt. Davis, 14th Pct.
Teeth: See dental	Shoes: Navy blue calf pump, with rhinestone crescent		Telegraph Bureau: Det./3rd Gr. P. Levine

chart in folder	Handbag Navy blue calf, sling strap	Bureau of Information Det./1st Gr. R. Nicholson
Scars	Luggage ?	Others
Appendectomy scar	Jewelry Worn Marley High School ring—class of June, 1939—worn on right ring finger	—
Deformities None		
Tattoo Marks None	Money Carried $4,375.00 believed to be withdrawn from Scranton bank	Notification to M.P. Bureau By: Det.-Lt. B. Raphael, 14th Detective Squad
Condition Physical Good Mental Good	Characteristics, Habits, Mannerisms —	Received at M.P. Bureau By: Sgt. L. Norris; Assigned — Squad —; Assigned Det./ M.P. Bur. 2nd Gr. John Phillips
Reported by Henry Proschek	Address 1112 Main, Scranton, Pa.	Telephone No. SC 2-7185 Relationship Father

Remarks Girl gave no indication she was leaving home. Was seen at train station next morning. Subsequent letter from this city (no return address) advised parents she had come here to start "a new life." Also said "longer letter will follow." (See letter in folder.) This was last contact parents had with girl. Father, in city week later, phoned 14th, nearest precinct.

Det. John Phillips — Signature of Assigned Detective

Lt. Samuel Barker — Commanding Officer

There were, Kling noticed, certain inconsistencies in the report. Early in the report, for example, the girl was "last seen at" her "home address" on October 31 at 11:45 P.M. Later in the report, under REMARKS, the girl was last seen at the Scranton railroad station the next morning. Kling surmised, as he was forced to surmise, that police procedure was responsible for the foul-up. Henry Proschek was the man who'd reported his daughter missing. And he had probably last seen her in his own home on the night of October 31. Someone else, apparently, had seen her at the railroad station the next morning, had observed her carefully enough to describe what she was wearing. But this someone else was not the person filing the complaint, hence the inconsistency. There was, Kling further noticed, a question mark under the word *luggage*. He wondered if she had, indeed, gone baggageless or if the observer at the station had simply failed to notice any luggage.

The report was somewhat vague when it said, "See letter in folder." Did this mean the first letter the girl had written or the longer letter she'd promised? And which of these letters was the last contact the parents had had? The answer, obviously, was in the folder.

Kling opened it again.

There was only one letter in the folder. Apparently, the second longer letter had never been written. And, apparently, it was this lack of further clarifying communication that had brought Henry Proschek to the city in search of his daughter, culminating in his phone call to the closest police station.

Feeling somewhat like a Peeping Tom, Kling began reading Mary Louise Proschek's letter to her parents:

November 1st

Dear Mom and Daddy:

I know your not worried I was kidnapped or anything because Betty Anders happened to spy me at the station this morning and by now it is probly all over town. So I know your not worried but I suppose you are wondering why I have left and when I am coming back.

I suppose I shouldn't have left without an explanation, but I don't think you would understand or improve what Im about to do. I have been planning on it for a long time, and it is something I have to do which is also why I have been staying on at Johnson's because I was saving my money all these years. I now have more than $4,000 dollars, you have to hand it to me for being persistint, ha ha.

I will write you a longer letter when everything here is settled. I am starting a new life here, Daddy, so please don't be too angry with me. Try to understand. Love and kisses.

Your loving dghtr,
Mary Louise

Whoever Detective Phillips of the Missing Persons Bureau was, he had done a good job on the missing Proschek girl. He had put a call through to the Scranton police, who had then checked with the girl's bank and discovered that $4,375 had been withdrawn from her account on October 31, the day before she'd left. The withdrawal slip had been signed by her and presented by her together with her passbook. Detective Phillips had then put a check on every bank in the city in an attempt to locate a new account started by Mary Louise Proschek. Each bank reported negatively. Phillips had checked on the stationery the girl used and found it to be five-and-dime stuff. The letter had been mailed special delivery and postmarked from a station in the heart of the city. A check had been made of hock shops in the hope the high school graduation ring would turn up. It had not. Phillips had acquired a dental chart from the girl's parents, and that was in her folder. Kling removed it and gave it a summary glance.

He remembered that the floater's lower front teeth had been lost in the water, but he couldn't remember which of her other teeth had fillings or which had been extracted. He sighed and turned to some of the other information in the folder.

The preliminary investigatory work had been handled by people other than the Missing Persons Bureau, of course. When Henry Proschek had reported his daughter's absence to the 14th Precinct, the detective he'd spoken to had immediately checked with the desk officer to ascertain whether or not Mary Louise had been either arrested or hospitalized in his precinct. He then checked with Communications and the Bureau of Information to find out if anyone answering her description was in a hospital or a morgue at the moment. When his efforts to locate her had proved fruitless, he had then phoned the information in to the MP Bureau, where the routine business of preparing forms

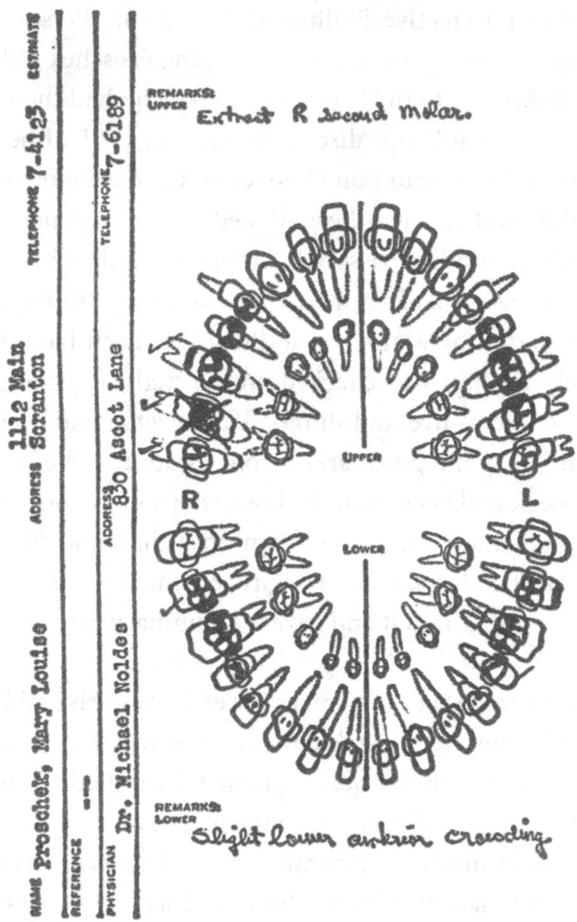

NAME Proschek, Mary Louise ADDRESS 1112 Main Scranton TELEPHONE 7-4123 ESTIMATE

REFERENCE

PHYSICIAN Dr. Michael Noldes ADDRESS 830 Ascot Lane TELEPHONE 7-6189

REMARKS: UPPER Extract R second molar.

UPPER

R L

LOWER

REMARKS: LOWER Slight lower anterior crowding.

in triplicate had then followed. And, to confirm his phone call, he mailed on the next day one of the triplicate copies of his own report to the MP Bureau.

The MP Bureau had sent out a teletype alarm throughout the city and to nearby police areas. And the name of Mary Louise Proschek had been added to the daily mimeographed list of missing persons that is distributed to transportation terminals, hospitals, and anyplace where a refugee might seek help or shelter.

The girl was still missing. Perhaps she was the 87th's floater.

But if Kling could remember very little about the floater's teeth, he could remember one important point about her right hand. There had been a tattoo on the flap of skin between the girl's right thumb and forefinger—the word *MAC* in a heart.

On Mary Louise Proschek's missing person report, under the heading TATTOOS, there was one word—and that word was "None."

Henry Proschek was a small, thin man with deep-brown eyes and a bald head. He was a coal miner, and the grime of three decades had permanently lodged beneath his fingernails and in the seams of his face. He was dressed in his Sunday best, and he had scrubbed himself vigorously before coming up from Scranton, but he still looked grubby, and if you didn't know his trade was the honest occupation of extracting coal from the earth, you would have considered him a dirty little man.

He sat in the squadroom of the 87th Precinct, and Carella watched him. There was indignation in Proschek's eyes, a flaring indignation that Carella had not thought the miner capable of. Proschek had just listened to Kling's little speech, and now there was indignation in his eyes, and Carella wondered whether or not Kling had delivered his talk wrong. He decided that Kling had done it in the only way possible. The kid was new, but he was learning, and there are only so many ways to tell a man his daughter is dead.

Proschek sat with his indignation in his eyes, and then his anger spread to his mouth and bubbled from his lips. "She's not dead," he said.

"She *is*, Mr. Proschek," Kling said. "Sir, I'm sorry, but—"

"She's not dead," Proschek said firmly.

"Sir—"

And, again, he said, "*She's not dead!*"

Kling turned to Carella. Carella shoved himself off the desk effortlessly. "Mr. Proschek," he said, "we've compared the dead girl's teeth with the dental chart you gave to the Missing Persons Bureau. They're identical, sir. Believe me, we wouldn't have had this happen—"

"There's been a mistake," Proschek said.

"There's been no mistake, sir."

"How could she be dead?" Proschek asked. "She came here to start a new life. She said so. She wrote that to me. So how could she be dead?"

"Her body—"

"And you wouldn't find my daughter drowned. My daughter was an excellent swimmer. My daughter won a medal in high school for her swimming. I don't know who that girl is, but she's not Mary Louise."

"Sir—"

"I'd have broke her neck if she wore a tattoo. You said this dead girl has a tattoo on her hand. My Mary Louise would never even have considered a thing like that."

"That's what we wanted to find out from you, sir," Carella said. "You told us she didn't have a tattoo. In that case, she must have acquired the tattoo in this city. We know she wasn't drowned, you see. She was dead before she entered the water. So if we can tie in the tattoo with—"

"That dead girl isn't my daughter," Proschek said. "You brought me all the way from Pennsylvania, and she isn't even my daughter. Why are you wasting my time? I had to lose a whole day just to come here."

"Sir," Carella said firmly, "that girl is your daughter. Please try to understand that." Proschek stared at him hostilely. "Did she have any friends named Mac?" Carella asked.

"None," Proschek said.

"MacDonald, MacDougall, MacMorrow, MacManus, Mac-Thing, Mac-Anything?"

"No."

"Are you certain?"

"My daughter didn't have many boyfriends," Proschek said. "She…she wasn't a very pretty girl. She had good coloring, fair, like her mother—blue eyes and blonde hair, that's a good combination—but she didn't…She wasn't very pretty. I…I used to feel sorry for her. A man…It doesn't matter if a man isn't good looking. But, to a girl, looks are everything. I used to feel sorry for her." He paused and looked up at Carella and then repeated, as if to clarify his earlier statements, "She wasn't very pretty, my daughter."

Carella looked down at Proschek, knowing the coal miner had used the past tense, knowing that the girl was already dead in Proschek's mind, and wondering why the man fought the knowledge now, fought the indisputable knowledge that his daughter was dead and had been dead for at least three months.

"Please think, Mr. Proschek," he said. "Did she ever mention anyone named Mac?"

"No," Proscheck said. "Why should Mary Louise mention a Mac? That girl isn't Mary Louise." He paused, got a sudden idea, and said, "I want to see that girl."

"We'd rather you didn't," Carella said.

"I want to see her. You say she's my daughter, and you show me dental charts, and that's all a lot of crap. I want to see that girl. I can tell you whether or not she's Mary Louise."

"Is that what you called her?" Carella asked. "Mary Louise?"

"That's what I baptized her. Mary Louise. Everybody else called her just plain Mary, but that wasn't the way I intended it. I intended it Mary Louise. That's a pretty name, isn't it? Mary Louise. Mary is too…plain." He blinked. "Too plain." He blinked again. "I want to see that girl. Where is that girl?"

"At the mortuary," Kling said.

"Then take me there. A relative's supposed to identify a…a body, isn't he? Isn't that the case?"

Kling looked at Carella.

"We'll check out a car and take Mr. Proschek to the hospital," Carella said wearily.

They did not talk much on the ride to the hospital. The three men sat on the front seat of the Mercury sedan, and the city burst with April greenery around them, but the inside of the car was curiously cheerless. They drove into the hospital parking lot, and Carella parked the police sedan in a space reserved for the hospital staff. Mr. Proschek blinked against the sunshine when he got out of the car. Then he followed Carella and Kling to the morgue.

The detectives did not have to identify themselves to the attendant. They had both been there many times before. They told the attendant the number they wanted, and then they followed him past the rows of doors set into the corridor wall, the small refrigerator doors behind each one of which was a corpse.

"We don't advise this, Mr. Proschek," Carella said. "Your daughter was in the water for a long time. I don't think—"

Proschek was not listening to him. They had stopped before a door marked 28, and Proschek was watching the attendant.

"Yes or no, Steve?" the attendant asked, reaching for the handle of the door.

Carella sighed. "Show it to him, buddy," he said, and the attendant opened the door and rolled out the slab.

Proschek looked at the decomposed, hairless body of the girl on the slab. Carella watched him, and for a brief second, he saw recognition leap into the coal miner's eyes, shocking, sudden recognition, and he felt some of the pain the old man was feeling.

And then Proschek turned to face Carella, and his eyes were like agate, and his mouth was set into a hard, tight line.

"No," he said. "She's not my daughter."

His words echoed down the long corridor. The attendant rolled the slab back into the refrigerator compartment, and the rollers squeaked.

"He claiming the body?" the attendant asked.

"Mr. Proschek?" Carella asked.

"What?" Proschek said.

"Are you claiming the body?"

"What?"

"Are you—"

"No," Proschek said. "She's not my daughter." He turned and started down the corridor, his heels clacking on the concrete floor. "She's not my daughter," he said, his voice rising. "She's not my daughter. She's not my daughter. She's not my daughter."

And then he reached the door at the end of the corridor, and he fell to his knees, his hand clutching the knob, and he began sobbing bitterly. Carella ran to him, and he stooped and put his arm around the old man, and Proschek buried his face in Carella's chest, weeping, and he said, "Oh my God, she's dead. My Mary Louise is dead. My daughter is dead. My daughter…" and then he couldn't say anything else because his body was trembling and his tears were choking him.

The beauty of being a shoemaker, Teddy Carella thought, is that you don't take your work home with you. You cobble so many shoes, and then you go home to your wife, and you don't think about soles and heels until the next day.

A cop thinks about heels all the time.

A cop like Steve Carella thinks about souls, too.

She would not, of course, have been married to anyone else, but it pained her nonetheless to see him sitting by the window brooding. His brooding position was almost classical, almost like the Rodin statue. He sat slumped in the easy chair, his chin cupped in one large hand, his legs crossed. He sat barefoot, and she loved his feet. *That's ridiculous. You don't love a man's feet. Well, the hell with you, I love his feet. They've got good clean arches and nice toes, so sue me*, she thought.

She walked to where he was sitting.

She was not a tall girl, but she somehow gave an impression of height. She held her head high, and her shoulders erect, and she walked lightly with a regal grace that added inches to her stature. Her hair was black, and her eyes were brown, and she wore no lipstick now on full lips, which needed none, anyway. The lips of Teddy Carella were decorative—decorative in that they were beautiful and decorative in that they could never form words. She had been born deaf, and she could neither hear nor speak, and so her entire face, her entire body, served as her means of communication.

Her face spoke in exaggerated syllables. Her eyes gave tongue to words she could not utter. Her hands moved fluidly, expressively, to convey meaning. When Teddy Carella listened, her eyes never left your face. When Teddy Carella "spoke," you were compelled to give her your complete attention because her pantomime somehow enhanced the delicacy of her loveliness.

Now, standing spread-legged before her brooding husband, she put her hands on her hips and stared down at him. She wore a red wraparound skirt, a huge gold safety pin fastening it just above her left knee. She wore red Capezio flats and a white blouse swooped low at the throat to the first swelling rise of her breasts. She had caught her hair back with a bright-red ribbon, and she stood before him now and defied him to continue with his sullen brooding.

Neither spoke—Teddy because she could not, and Carella because he would not. The silent skirmish filled the small apartment.

At last, Carella said, "All right, all right."

Teddy nodded and cocked one eyebrow.

"Yes," he said, "I'm emerging from my shell."

She hinged her hands together at the wrist and opened them slowly and then snapped them shut.

"You're right," Carella said. "I'm a clam."

She pointed a pistol-finger at him and squeezed the trigger.

"Yes, my work," he said.

Abruptly, without warning, she moved onto his lap. His arms circled her, and she cuddled up into a warm ball, pulling her knees up, snuggling her head against his chest. She looked up at him, and her eyes said, *Tell me.*

"This girl," he said. "Mary Louise Proschek."

Teddy nodded.

"Thirty-three years old, comes to the city to start a new life. Turns up floating in the Harb. Letter to her folks was full of good spirits. Even if we suspected suicide, which we don't, the letter would fairly well eliminate that. The ME says she was dead before she hit the water. Cause of death was acute arsenic poisoning. You following me?"

Teddy nodded, her eyes wide.

"She's got a tattoo mark right here"—he showed the spot on his right hand—"the word *MAC* in a heart. Didn't have it when she left Scranton, her hometown. How many Macs do you suppose there are in this city?"

Teddy rolled her eyes.

"You said it. Did she come here to meet this Mac? Did she just run into him by accident? Is he the one who threw her in the river after poisoning her? How do you go about locating a guy named Mac?"

Teddy pointed to the flap of skin between her thumb and forefinger.

"The tattoo parlors? I've already started checking them. We may get a break because not many women wear tattoos."

Quickly, Teddy unbuttoned the top button of her blouse and then pulled it open, using both hands, spreading it in a wide, dramatic V.

"The Rose Tattoo?" Carella asked. "That's fiction."

Teddy shrugged.

Carella grinned. "Besides, I think you just wanted an excuse to bare your bosom."

Teddy shrugged again, impishly.

"Not that it isn't a lovely bosom."

Teddy's eyebrows wagged seductively. She curved her hands through the air and moistened her lips.

"Of course," Carella said, "I've seen better."

Oh? Teddy's face asked, suddenly coldly aloof.

"There was this girl in burlesque," Carella expanded. "She could set them going in opposite directions, one swinging to the right, the other to the left. Had a little light on each one. They'd turn out all the houselights, and you'd just see these two circles of light in the darkness. Fantastic!" He grinned at his wife. "Now, that's what I call talent."

Teddy shrugged, telling her husband that that was what she didn't call any talent whatsoever.

"You, on the other hand…" His hand came up suddenly to cup her breast.

Gingerly, delicately, Teddy picked up his hand with her thumb and forefinger and deposited it on the arm of the chair.

"Angry?" Carella asked.

Teddy shook her head.

"Love me?" Carella asked.

Teddy shook her head most vigorously.

"Hate me?"

No.

"Who then?"

Teddy swung her forefingers in opposite directions, and Carella burst out laughing. "You hate the burlesque dancer?"

Teddy gave one emphatic nod.

"I don't blame you," he said. "She was an old bag."

Teddy beamed and threw her arms around his neck.

"Now do you love me?"

Yes, yes, yes.

"What'd you do all day?" he asked, holding her close, beginning to relax, succumbing to the warmth of her.

Teddy opened her hands like a book.

"Read?" Carella watched while she nodded. "What'd you read?"

Teddy scrambled off his lap and then clutched her middle, indicating that she had read something that was very funny. She walked across the room, and he watched her when she stooped alongside the magazine rack.

"If you're not careful," he said, "I'm going to undo that damn safety pin."

She put the magazines on the floor, stood up, and undid the safety pin. The skirt hung loose, one flap over the other. When she stooped to pick up the magazine again, it opened in a wide slit from her knee to almost her waist. Wiggling like the burlesque queen Carella had described, she walked back to him and dumped the magazines in his lap.

"Pen pal magazines?" Carella asked, astonished.

Teddy hunched up her shoulders, grinned, and then covered her mouth with one hand.

"My God!" he said. "Why?"

With her hands on her hips, Teddy kicked at the ceiling with one foot, the skirt opening over the clean line of her leg.

"For kicks?" Carella asked, shrugging. "What kind of stuff is in here? '*Dear Pen Pal: I am a cocker spaniel who always wanted to be in the movies...*'"

Teddy grinned and opened one of the magazines for him. Carella thumbed through it. She sat on the arm of his chair, and the skirt opened again. He looked at the magazine, and then he looked at his woman, and then he said, "The hell with this noise," and he threw the magazine to the floor and pulled Teddy onto his lap.

The magazine fell open to the personals column.

It lay on the floor while Steve Carella kissed his wife. It lay on the floor when he picked her up and carried her into the next room.

There was a small ad in the personals column.

It read:

Widower. Mature. Attractive. 35 years old. Seeks alliance with understanding woman of good background. Write P.O. Box 137.

The girl had read the advertisement six times, and she was now on her fifth revision of the letter she was writing in answer to it.

She was not a stupid girl, nor did she particularly believe anything romantic or exciting would happen after she mailed her letter. She was, after all, thirty-seven years old, and she had come to believe—once she'd turned thirty-five—that romance and excitement would never be a part of her life.

There was, in the girl's mind, a certain cynicism. There were some who would call her cynicism a simple case of sour grapes, but she honestly believed it was a good deal more than that. She had been weaned on the Big Romance legend, had had it bleated at her in radio serials, flashed before her eyes at the local movie house, seen it and heard it since she was old enough to understand the English language. She had been more susceptible to the legend because she was a girl—and a rather imaginative girl, at that. For her, the knight in shining armor *did* exist, and she would wait until he came along.

When you're not so pretty, the waiting can take a long time.

"Marty" is a nice-enough fiction, but the girls outnumber the men in this world of ours, and not many people care whether or not you can do differential calculus so long as you've got a beautiful phizz. Besides, she couldn't do differential calculus. Nor had she ever considered herself a particularly intelligent girl. She had gone to business school and scraped through, and she was a fair-enough secretary at a small hardware concern, and she was convinced at the age of thirty-seven that the Big Romance legend that had been foisted upon her by the fiction con men was just a great big crock.

She didn't mind it being a great big crock.

She told herself she didn't mind.

She had said good-bye to her virginity when she turned twenty-nine. She had been disappointed. No trumpets blasting, no banners unfurling, no clamorous medley of gonging bells. Just pain. Since that time, she had dabbled. She considered sex the periodic gratification of a purely natural urge. She approached sex with the paradoxical relentlessness of an uncaged jungle beast and the precise aloofness of a Quaker bride. Sex was like sleep. You needed both, but you didn't spend your life in bed.

And now, at thirty-seven, long since her parents had given up all hope for her, long since she herself had abandoned the Big Romance, the Wedding in June, the Honeymoon at Lovely Lake Lewis legend, she felt lonely.

She kept her own apartment, primarily because her jousting with sex would never have been understood by her parents, partly because she wanted complete independence—and alone in the apartment, she could hear the creaking of the floor boards and the unrelenting drip of the water tap, and she knew complete aloneness.

It is a big world.

From somewhere out in that big world, a mature attractive man of thirty-five sought an alliance with an understanding woman of good background.

Cut and dried, cold and impersonal, stripped of all the fictional hoop-dee-dah. The man could have been advertising for a Pontiac convertible or a slightly used power mower. She supposed it was this directness of approach that appealed to her. Understanding. Could she understand his appeal? Could she understand his loneliness, the single cipher in a teeming world of matched and mismatched couples? She thought she could. She thought she could detect honesty in his simple appeal.

And because she detected honesty there, her own dishonesty left her feeling somewhat guilty. This was the fifth draft of her letter, and her age had changed with each draft. In the first letter, she'd claimed to be thirty. The second letter advanced her age by two years. The third letter went back to thirty again. Number four admitted to thirty-one. She had done a bit of soul-searching before starting on the fifth rewrite.

He was, when you considered it, thirty-five. But he'd said he was mature. A mature man of thirty-five isn't a college kid with a briar pipe. A mature man of thirty-five wanted and needed a woman of understanding. Could this not mean a woman who was slightly older than he, a woman who could…mother him? Sort of? Besides, wasn't complete honesty essential at this stage of the game? Especially with this man whose plea was devoid of all frills and fripperies?

But thirty-seven sounded so close to forty.

Who wants a forty-year-old spinster? (Should she mention that she was wise in the ways of the world?)

Thirty-three, on the other hand, sounded too suburban housewife—skirt and blouse and nylons and loafers, going to meet the 6:10. Was that what he wanted? A scatterbrained little blonde who hopped into the station wagon in compliance with the Commuter Romance legend—the automaton who set the roast according to her husband's train schedule? The robot who had the shaker full of martinis waiting for dear, tired, old hubby: *Hard day at the mine today, sweetheart?*

Or was he looking for the sleeker model? The silver-toned beauty in the red Thunderbird rushing over country lanes. Gray flannel pedal-pushers, white blouse, bright-red scarf at the throat, push-button control, push-pull-click-click: *Dahling, we're terribly late for the Samalsons. Do tie your tie.*

He wanted honesty.

I am thirty-six years old, she wrote.

Well, almost honesty.

She crossed out the words. This man deserved complete honesty. She tore up the fifth letter, picked up the pen, and in a neat, precise hand—except for the *t*'s, which were crossed with somewhat animalistic ferocity—she began writing her letter again:

Dear Sir:

I am thirty-seven years old.

I start my letter with this fact because I do not wish to waste your time. Your appeal seemed, to me, an honest one—and so I am being completely honest in return. I am thirty-seven. This is the fact of the matter. If you are now tearing up this letter and throwing it into the waste basket, so be it.

You asked for an understanding woman. I ask for an understanding man. It is not easy to write this letter. I can imagine how difficult it was for you to place your ad, and

I can understand what led you to do so. I can only ask for the same understanding on your part.

I felt almost as if I were applying for a position somewhere. I don't want to feel that way, but I can see no other way of letting you know what I am like and I wish (if you decide to answer my letter) that you will follow the same pattern. I am going to tell you what I am, and who I am.

Physically, I am five-feet-four inches tall. I am one hundred and ten pounds without dieting. I mention that because I'm not one of these women who have to watch everything they eat. I always stay slim. I've been the same weight, give or take a few pounds, for the longest time. I can still wear skirts I bought when I was twenty-one.

My hair is brown, and my eyes are brown. I wear glasses. I had to start wearing them when I was twelve because I ruined my eyes reading so much. I don't read very much anymore. I've become disillusioned with fiction, and the non-fiction is either inspirational stuff or stuff about mountain climbing, and I neither want to be inspired nor do I desire to climb Everest. I thought for a while that foreign novels might offer me something American novels didn't—but everyone is selling the same thing these days, and the product usually suffers in translation. Perhaps you've run across some reading which I haven't discovered yet, and which could offer me the deep pleasure I got from books when I was a little girl. If so, I'd appreciate knowing about it.

I dress quietly. The brightest dress I own is a yellow taffeta, and I haven't worn that for ages. I usually prefer suits. I work in an office, you see, and it's a somewhat staid place. I have a lot of clothes, incidentally, which I've accumulated over the years. I wouldn't call myself exactly penniless, either.

I'm a secretary, and I've been earning close to ninety dollars a week for a long time. Twenty of that I send to my parents, but the remaining seventy or so is more than enough to keep me going. This may sound ridiculously businesslike, but I do have almost five thousand dollars in the bank, and I'd honestly like to know what your financial setup is, too.

My tastes are simple. I like good music. I don't mean Rock and Roll. I've sort of outgrown the candy stick and dungaree set. I like Brahms and I like Wagner-Wagner especially. There is something wild in his music, and I find it exciting. I like pop music on the sentimental side. I don't mean the current hit parade rages. I mean old standards done up in albums. Stuff like Smoke Gets In Your Eyes *and* Stardust *and* This Love Of Mine, *you get the idea. I think my favorite record album is Sinatra's* In The Wee Small Hours. *I've always liked him, and whatever his trouble with Ava Gardner, it's none of my business. I listen to records a lot. Living alone can be too quiet. I play my albums at night, and they help to pass the time.*

I generally sew while I'm listening. I'm a good seamstress and I've made many of my own clothes. I hate darning socks. I feel I should tell you that right now. I feel I should also tell you that my indoor activities are not confined to playing records alone.

(She stopped here, wondering if she had said too much, wondering if she sounded too bold. Would he understand what she meant? A widower couldn't possibly want a girl with absolutely no experience! Still…)

I do a lot of other things indoors. Like cooking. And other things. I'm a good cook. I can make potatoes forty-two different ways. I'm not exaggerating, and my specialty is Southern fried chicken, though I have never been down South. My ambition is to travel around the United States someday. I half think that's why I've been saving my money so religiously.

Oh...religion.

I'm Protestant.

I hope you're Protestant, too, but it really doesn't matter that much. I hope you're white, too, because I am and that would matter to me—not that I'm prejudiced or anything. Honestly, I'm not. But I'm too mature to be defiant, and I don't feel like battling the good fight for democracy, not at this late stage of the game. I hope you understand this isn't bigotry. It's caution, it's fear, it's wanting to belong, it's whatever you choose to call it. But it's not bigotry.

I ride a little, usually in the Spring and in the Fall. I like the outdoors, though I'm not a very good athlete. I swim pretty well. I have a fast crawl. I was once a swimming counselor at a children's camp, and I learned to dislike children that Summer. Of course, I've never had any of my own so I wouldn't know. I imagine it's different with your own. You said you are a widower. Do you have any children?

So far, you are just a post office box number, and here I've told you almost everything I could think of about myself. I like movies. John Wayne is my favorite. He's not very good-looking, but there is a manliness about him, and I think that's very important.

Well, I suppose that's it.

I hope you'll answer this letter. I'll send you a picture if you like after I hear from you again. I say "again," because I feel by reading your ad I've already heard from you once.

And I honestly feel I did "hear" you, if you know what I mean.

Sincerely,
Priscilla Ames
41 La Mesa Street
Phoenix, Arizona

Priscilla Ames read her letter over. It seemed honest and sincere to her. She had no desire to make herself sound more attractive than she really was. Why start out with a bunch of lies and then get tangled up in them later? No, this was the best way.

Priscilla Ames folded the letter—which ran to some six pages—and then put it into the envelope. She copied the address from the magazine onto the face of the envelope, sealed the envelope, and then went out to mail it.

Priscilla Ames didn't know what she was asking for.

It's the little things in life that get you down.

The big problems are the easy ones to solve. There's a lot at stake with the big problems. It's the little ones that are the tough bastards. Should I shave tonight for the big date with Buxom Blonde, or should I wait until tomorrow morning for the big conference with Amalgamated Aluminum? God, a man can go nuts!

The 87th's big problem was the floater. It's not often you get a floater.

The 87th's little problem was the con man.

It was the con man who was driving Detective Arthur Brown nuts. Brown didn't like to be conned, and he didn't like other people to be conned, either. The man—or men, more accurately—who were fleecing honest citizens of Brown's fair city rankled him. They invaded his sleep. They dulled his appetite. They were even ruining his sex life. He was surly and out of sorts, more impatient than ever, scowling, snapping, a very difficult man to work with. The men who worked with him, being kindly, considerate, thoughtful bulls, did everything in their power to make his working day even more difficult. A moment did not go by but what one or another of the 87th's bulls would make some passing crack to Brown about the difficulties he was experiencing with the con man.

"Catch him yet, Artie?" they would ask.

"Hey, some guy conned my grandmother out of her false teeth yesterday," they would say. "Think it's your buzzard, Brown?"

Brown took all the patter and all the jive with enviable discourteousness, admirable lack of self-control, and remarkable short temper. His usual answer was short and to the point and consisted of a combination of two words, one of which was unprintable. Brown had no time for jokes. He only had time for the files.

Somewhere in those files was the man he wanted.

Bert Kling was occupied with another kind of reading matter.

Bert Kling stood before the bulletin board in the detective squadroom. It was raining again, and the rain oozed against the windowpanes, and the harsh light behind the panes cast a sliding, running, dripping silhouette on the floor at his feet so that the room itself seemed to be slowly dissolving.

The vacations schedule had been posted on the bulletin board.

Kling studied it now. Two detectives studied it with him. One of the detectives was Meyer Meyer. The other was Roger Havilland.

"What'd you draw, kid?" Havilland asked.

"June tenth," Kling replied.

"June tenth? Well, well, well, ain't that a dandy time to start a holiday?" Havilland said, winking at Meyer.

"Yeah, dandy," Kling said disgustedly. He had honestly not expected a choicer spot. He was the newest man on the squad—promoted from a rookie, at that—and so he could hardly have hoped to compete with the cops who had seniority. But he was nonetheless disappointed. June 10! Hell, that wasn't even summer yet!

"I like my vacations at the early part of June," Havilland went on. "Excellent time for vacations. I always ask for the end of April. I like it chilly. I wouldn't think of leaving this lovely squadroom during the suffocating months of July and August. I like heat, don't you, Meyer?"

Meyer's blue eyes twinkled. He was always willing to go along with a gag, even when the gag originated with a man like Havilland whom Meyer did not particularly like. "Heat is wonderful," Meyer said. "Last year was marvelous. I'll never forget last year. A cop hater loose and the temperature in the nineties. That makes for a memorable summer."

"Just think, kid," Havilland said. "Maybe this summer'll be a hot one, too. You can sit over there by the windows, where you get a nice breeze from the park. And you can think back over your nice cool vacation in the beginning of June."

"You slay me, Havilland," Kling said. He turned to start away from the bulletin board, and Havilland laid a beefy hand on his arm. There was strength in Havilland's fingers. He was a big cop with a cherubic face, and a leer-like smile was on that face now. Kling disliked Havilland. He had disliked him even when he'd been a patrolman and had only heard of Havilland's questioning tactics with suspects. Since he'd made 3rd/grade, he had had the opportunity to see Havilland in action, and his dislike had mounted in proportion to the number of times Havilland used his ham like fists on helpless prisoners. Havilland, you see, was a bull. He roared like a bull, and he gored like a bull, and he probably even snored like a bull. In truth, he had once been a gentle cop. But he'd once tried to break up a street fight, and the fighters had ganged up on him, taken away his service revolver, and broken his arm with a lead pipe. The compound fracture had to be broken and reset at the hospital. It healed painfully and slowly. It left Havilland with a philosophy: Hit first; ask later.

The broken arm, to Kling's way of thinking, bought neither benediction nor salvation for Havilland. Neither did it buy understanding. It bought, perhaps, a little bit of insight into a man who was basically a son of a bitch. Kling wasn't a psychiatrist. He only knew that he didn't like the leer on Havilland's face, and he didn't like Havilland's hand on his arm.

"Where you going on your vacation, kid?" Havilland asked. "You don't want to waste that nice cool month of June, do you? Remember, it gets to be summer along about the twenty-first. Where you going, huh?"

"We haven't decided yet," Kling said.

"We? *We*? You going with somebody?"

"I'm going with my fiancée," Kling said tightly.

"Your girl, huh?" Havilland said. He winked at Meyer, including him in a secret fraternity that Meyer did not feel like joining.

"Yes," Kling said. "My girl."

"Whatever you do," Havilland said, winking at Kling this time, "don't take her out of the state."

"Why not?" Kling asked, the implication escaping him for a moment, immediately sorry as soon as Havilland opened his mouth in reply.

"Why, the Mann Act, kid!" Havilland said. "Watch out for those state lines."

Kling stared at Havilland and then said, "How would you like a punch in the mouth, Havilland?"

"Oh, Jesus!" Havilland roared. "The kid breaks me up! There's nothing dishonest about screwing, kid, unless you cross a state line!"

"Lay off, Rog," Meyer said.

"What's the matter?" Havilland asked. "I envy the kid. Vacation in June, and a sweet little shack-up waiting for—"

"Lay off!" Meyer said, more loudly this time. He had seen the spark of sudden anger in Kling's eyes, and he had seen the involuntary clenching of Kling's right fist. Havilland outweighed and outreached Kling, and Havilland was not famous for the purity of his fighting tactics. Meyer did not want blood on the squadroom floor—not Kling's blood, anyway.

"Nobody's got any sense of humor in this dump," Havilland said surlily. "You got to have a sense of humor here, or you don't survive."

"Go help Brown with his con man troubles," Meyer said.

"Brown ain't got no humor, either," Havilland said, and he stalked off.

"That big turd," Kling said. "Someday…"

"Well," Meyer said, his eyes twinkling, "in a sense, he's right. The Mann Act is a serious thing. Very serious."

Kling looked at him. Meyer had used almost the same words as Havilland, but somehow, there was a difference. "A very serious thing," he answered. "I'll be careful, Meyer."

"Caution is the watchword," Meyer said, grinning.

"The truth is," Kling said, "this damn June tenth spot might screw things up. Claire goes to college, you know. She may be in the middle of finals or something right then."

"You been planning on this for some time?" Meyer asked.

"Yeah," Kling said, thinking of the June 10 spot, and hoping it would jibe with Claire's schedule, and wondering what he could do about it if it didn't.

Meyer nodded sympathetically. "Is it a special occasion?" he asked. "Your going away together, I mean?"

Kling, immersed in his thoughts, answered automatically, forgetting he was talking to a fellow cop. "Yes," he said. "We're in love."

"The trouble with you," Havilland said to Brown, "is you're in love with your work."

"I spend almost all my waking hours in this room," Brown said. "It'd be a sad goddamn thing if I didn't like what I was doing."

"It wouldn't be sad at all," Havilland said. "I hate being a cop."

"Then why don't you quit the force?" Brown asked flatly.

"They need me too much," Havilland said.

"Sure."

"They do. This squad would go to pieces in a week if I wasn't around to hold its hand."

"Hold this a while," Brown said.

"Crime would flourish," Havilland continued, unfazed. "The city would be overrun by cheap thieves."

"Roger Havilland, Protector of the People," Brown said.

"That's me," Havilland confessed.

"Here, Protector," Brown said, "take a look at this."

"What?"

"This RKC card. How does it look to you?"

"What am I supposed to be looking for?" Havilland asked.

"A con man," Brown said. He handed the card to Havilland.

With the casual scrutiny born of years of detective work, Havilland studied the face of the card:

RESIDENT KNOWN CRIMINAL

Name Frederick Deutsch Command 2
Alias Fritzie, Dutch, The Dutchman
Address 67 South 4th Street Precinct 87th
Floor 1st Apartment No. 1C House ——

CHANGE OF ADDRESS

Moved to Hotel Carter, Culver and
South 11th
Criminal Specialty Confidence man
Names of Associates —— Prison (In or Out) Out

D.D. 64b Note—If criminal moves, forward card to Resident Precinct. (Over)

"Tells me nothing," Havilland said.

"Flip it over," Brown told him.

Havilland turned over the card and began reading again.

Gallery No. 73471-3R **DESCRIPTION**

Where born U.S.A.
Sex Male Age 31 Color White
Eyes Blue Hair Brown Ht. 5'11¼"
Weight 145 Occup. Waiter
Right- or Left-Handed Right
Distinctive Marks or Scars Small
scar under chin
Operator or Chauffeur License Operator
Automobile License No. 7295-BN Model 1954
Make Nash Color Red and black

REMARKS Young but highly skilled in all confidence games. M.O. varies with each game. Operates alone or in pair, but partner never apprehended. Served 18 mos., released 1951.

"Could be," Havilland said.

"Thing that interests me about him is that he's a jack of all trades," Brown said. "You get a con man, he usually sticks to one game if it's working for him. This guy varies his game. Like the louse we got roaming the 87th. He must be pretty smooth, too, because he's barely a kid and he only took one fall." Brown looked at the card. "Who the hell made out this thing? It's supposed to tell you where he was sentenced and what for."

"What difference does it make?" Havilland asked airily.

"I like to know what I'm dealing with," Brown said.

"Why?"

"Because I'm heading for the Hotel Carter right now to pick him up."

The Hotel Carter was, in many respects, a very sleazy dump.

On the other hand, to those of its inhabitants who had recently arrived from skid row, it had all the glamour and impressiveness of the Waldorf Astoria. It all depended how you looked at it.

If you stood on the sidewalk at the corner of Culver Avenue and South Eleventh Street, and it happened to be raining, and you happened to be a cop out to make a pinch, the Hotel Carter looked like a very sleazy dump.

Brown sighed, pulled up the collar of his trench coat, remarked to himself silently that he looked something like a private eye, and then walked into the hotel lobby. An old man sat in a soiled easy chair looking out at the rain, remembering kisses from Marjorie Morningstar under the lilacs. The lobby smelled. Brown suspected the old man contributed to the smell. He adjusted his nostrils the way he would adjust his shoulder holster, glanced around quickly, and then walked to the desk.

The clerk watched him as he crossed the lobby. The clerk watched him carefully. An April fly, not yet feeling its summer oats, buzzed lazily around the desk. A brass spittoon at the base of the desk dripped with misaimed spittle. The smell in the lobby was a smell of slovenliness and dissolution. Brown reached the desk. He started to open his mouth.

"I'll give it to you straight," the desk clerk said. "We don't take niggers."

Brown didn't even blink. "You don't, huh?" he asked.

"We don't." The clerk was a young man, his hairline receding even though he was not yet twenty-six. He had a hawkish nose and pale-green eyes. An acne pimple festered near his right nose flap. "Nothing personal," he said. "I only work here, and those are the orders."

"Glad to know how you feel," Brown said, smiling. "Trouble is, I didn't ask."

"Huh?" the clerk said.

"Now, you have to understand there's nothing I'd like better than a room in this hotel. I just come up from a cotton patch down South where we fertilize our cotton with human excrement. I lived in a leaky tarpaper shack, and so you can imagine what a palace your fine, splendid hotel looks like to me. I think it would be too much for me to bear just being allowed to stay in one of your rooms. Why, just being here in the lobby is like coming close to paradise."

"Go ahead," the clerk said, "make wise cracks. You still don't get a room. I'm being honest with you. You should thank me."

"Oh, I do, I do," Brown said. "I thank you from the bottom of my cotton-pickin' heart. Is there a man named Frederick Deutsch registered here?"

"Who wants to know?" the clerk asked.

Brown smiled and sweetly said, "*I* want to know. Jus' li'l ol' cotton-pickin' me." He reached into his back pocket and flipped his wallet open to his shield. The clerk blinked. Brown continued smiling.

"I was only joking about the room," the clerk said. "We got lots of Negro people staying here."

"I'll bet the place is just packed with them," Brown said. "Is Deutsch registered here, or isn't he?"

"The name don't ring a bell," the clerk said. "He a transient?"

"A regular," Brown said.

"I got no Deutsches in my regulars."

"Let's see the list."

"Sure, but there aint a Deutsch on it. I know my steadies by heart."

"Let's see it anyway, huh?" Brown said.

The clerk sighed, dug under the counter, and came up with a register. He turned it on the desktop so that Brown could see it. Rapidly, Brown ran his finger down the page.

"Who's Frank Darren?" he asked.

"Huh?"

"Frank Darren." Brown pointed at the name. "This one."

"Oh." The clerk shrugged. "A guy. One of the guests."

"How long's he been here?"

"Couple years now, I guess. Even more than that."

"He register as Darren when he checked in?"

"Sure."

"What's he look like?"

"Tall guy, kind of skinny. Blue eyes, long hair. Why?"

"He in now?"

"I think so, yeah. Why?"

"What room's he in?"

"312," the clerk said. "I thought you was looking for somebody named Deutsch?"

"I am," Brown said. "Give me the key to 312."

"What for? You need a warrant before you go busting in on—"

"If I have to go all the way home for a warrant," Brown said levelly, "I'll also pick up one for violation of PL 514, excluding a citizen by reason of color from the equal enjoyment of any accommodation furnished by innkeepers or—"

Hastily, the clerk handed him the key. Brown nodded and crossed to the elevator. He stabbed at the button and waited patiently while the elevator crept down to the lobby. When it opened, a blonde chambermaid stepped out of it, winking at the elevator operator.

"Three," Brown said.

The elevator operator stared at him. "Did you see the clerk?"

"I saw the clerk, and the clerk saw me. Now, let's cut the bull and get this car in motion."

The elevator operator stepped back, and Brown entered the car. He leaned back against the back wall as the car climbed. Darren, of course, might very well be Darren and not Deutsch, he reasoned. But an elementary piece of police knowledge was that a man registering under a phony name—especially if his luggage, shirts, or handkerchiefs were monogrammed—would generally pick a name with the same initials as his real name. Frederick Deutsch, Frank Darren—it was worth a try. Besides, the RKC card had given this as Deutsch's last address. Maybe the card was wrong. Or, if it was right, why hadn't the mastermind who'd figured out where Deutsch was staying also have mentioned the fact that he was registered under an alias? Brown did not like sloppy police work. Sloppiness made him impatient. Slow elevators also made him impatient.

When they reached the third floor, he said, "Doesn't it hurt your eardrums?"

"Doesn't what hurt my eardrums?" the elevator operator asked.

"Breaking the sound barrier like this?" Brown said, and then he stepped into the corridor. He waited until the doors slid shut behind him. He looked at the two doors closest to him in the corridor, to ascertain which way the numbers were running, and then he turned right.

302, 304, 306, 308, 310…

He stopped outside room 312 and reached under his coat. He pulled the .38 from its shoulder rig, thumbed off the safety, and then took the key the clerk had given him and inserted it into the latch with his left hand.

Inside the room, there was sudden movement. Brown turned the key quickly and kicked open the door. There was a man on the bed, and the man was in the process of reaching for a gun that lay on the night table.

"Better leave it where it is," Brown said.

"What is this?" the man asked. He was somewhat better looking than his photo, but not much. He looked a little older, possibly because the photo had been taken many years back when he'd been mugged and printed before his arraignment. He wore a white-on-white shirt open at the throat, the sleeves rolled up just past his wrists, bulging with the cuff links, which had been rolled up with the material. A small monogram was on the man's left breast pocket, the red letters FD in a black diamond.

"Put on your coat," Brown said. "I want to talk to you back at the squad."

"What about?"

"Swindling," Brown said.

"You can just blow it out," the man said.

"Can I?"

"Damn right you can. I'm as legitimate as the Virgin Mary."

"Is that why you carry a gun?" Brown asked.

"I've got a permit," the man said.

"We'll check that back at the precinct, too."

"Go get a warrant for my arrest," the man said.

"I don't need any goddamn warrant!" Brown snapped. "Now, get the hell off that bed and into your coat, or I'll have to help you. And you won't like my help, believe me."

"Listen, what the hell—"

"Come on, Fritzie," Brown said.

The man looked up sharply.

"It is Fritzie, isn't it?" Brown asked. "Or is it Dutch?"

"My name's Frank Darren," the man said.

"And mine's Peter Pan. Put on your coat."

"You're making a mistake, pal," the man said. "I've got friends."

"A judge?" Brown asked. "A senator? What?"

"Friends," the man said.

"I got friends, too," Brown said. "I got a good friend who runs a butcher shop in Diamondback. He'll be as much help to you as your judge. Now, come on, we're wasting time."

The man slid off the bed. "I got nothing to hide," he said. "You got nothing on me."

"I hope not," Brown said. "I hope you're clean, and I hope you've got a permit for that gun, and I hope you went to confession last week. In the meantime, let's go back to the precinct."

"Jesus, can't we talk here?" the man asked.

"No," Brown said. He grinned. "They don't allow niggers in this hotel."

The man's license and registration were made out to Frederick Deutsch.

Brown looked them over and said, "All right, why were you registered under an alias?"

"You wouldn't understand," Deutsch said.

"Try me."

"What the hell for. I'm innocent until I'm proved guilty. Is there any law against using a phony name to register in a hotel?"

"As a matter of fact," Brown said, "it's a misdemeanor, violation of PL 964. Use of name or address with intent to deceive."

"I wasn't trying to deceive anybody," Deutsch said.

"I can get a court injunction without any proof that you've deceived and misled anybody."

"So get one," Deutsch said.

"What for? I don't care if you use the name forever. I'd just like to know why you felt it was necessary to hide behind an alias."

"You hit it, cop," Deutsch said.

"If I hit it, I don't know it," Brown answered. "What's the story?"

"I'm going straight," Deutsch said.

"Hold it a minute," Brown said. "Let me get the string quartet in here. We're going to need violins for this one."

"I told you you wouldn't understand," Deutsch said, wagging his head.

Brown studied him seriously for a moment. "Go ahead," he said. "I'm listening."

"I took a fall in 1950," Deutsch said. "I was twenty-four years old. I'd been working the confidence game since I was seventeen. First time I fell. I got off with eighteen months. On Walker Island." Deutsch shrugged.

"So?"

"So I didn't like it. Is that so hard to understand? I didn't like being cooped up. Eighteen months with every kind of crazy bastard you could imagine. Queers and winos and junkies and guys who'd ax their own mothers. Eighteen months of it. When I got out, I'd had it. I'd had it, and I didn't want anymore of it."

"So?"

"So I decided to play it straight. I figured I take another fall, it ain't going to be eighteen months this time. This time it'll be a little longer. The third time, who knows? Maybe they throw away the key. Maybe they begin to figure Fritzie Deutsch is just another guy like these queers and winos and junkies."

"But you weren't," Brown said, a faint smile on his mouth.

"No, I wasn't. I conned a lot of people, but I was a gent, and you can go to hell if you don't believe me. Working the game was the same as having a job with me. That's why I got so good at it."

"I imagine it paid pretty well, too," Brown said.

"I'm still wearing the clothes I bought when things were going good," Deutsch said. "But what's the percentage? A few years of good living, and the rest of my life cooped up with slobs? Is that what I wanted? That's what I asked myself. So I decided to straighten out."

"I'm listening."

"It ain't so easy," Deutsch said, sighing. "Guys don't want ex-cons working for them. I know that sounds corny as hell. I see it in a lot of movies, even. Where Robert Taylor or somebody can't get a job because he once was a con. Only, of course, with him, it's like he was a con by mistake. You know, he took the fall when he was really clean. Anyway, it's true. It's tough to get a job when you got a record. They make a few phone calls, and they find out Fritzie Deutsch done time...Well, so long Fritzie, it's been nice knowing you."

"So you assumed the Frank Darren alias, is that right?"

"Yeah," Deutsch said.

"And you've got a job now?"

"I work in a bank."

"Doing what?"

"I'm a guard." Deutsch looked up quickly to see if Brown was smiling. Brown was not. "That's how come I've got a permit for the gun," Deutsch added. "I ain't snowing you. That's one thing you can check."

"We can check a lot of things," Brown said. "What bank do you work for?"

"You going to tell them my real name?" Deutsch asked. A sudden fear had come into his eyes, and he put his hand on Brown's arm, and the fingers there were tense and tight.

"No," Brown said.

"First National. The Mason Avenue branch."

"I'll check that, and I'll check the permit," Brown said. "But there's one other thing."

"What?"

"I want some mooches to meet you."

"What for? I ain't conned anybody since—"

"They may think differently. If you're clean, you won't mind them looking you over."

"At the lineup? Jesus, do I have to go to the lineup?"

"No. I'll ask the victims to come down here."

"I'm clean," Deutsch said. "I got nothing to worry about. It's just I hate the lineup."

"Why?"

Deutsch looked up at Brown, and his eyes were wide and serious. "It's full of bums, you know that?" He paused and sucked in a deep breath. "And I ain't a bum anymore."

Murder will out, and it was a fine day for the outing of murder. The fiction con men could not have chosen a better day. They would have written it just this way, with the rain a fine-drilling drizzle that swept in over the River Harb, and the sky an ominous, roiling gray behind it. The tugboats on the river moaned occasionally, and the playgrounds on the other side of the River Highway were empty, the black asphalt glistening slickly under the steady wash of the rain. The movie con men would have panned their cameras down over the empty silent playgrounds, across the concrete of the River Highway, down the slopes of the embankments leading to the river. The sound track would pick up the wail of the tugs and the sullen swish of the rain and the murmur of the river lapping at rotted wooden beams.

There would be a close-up, and the close-up would show a hand suddenly breaking the surface of the water, the fingers stiff and widespread.

And then a body would appear, and the water would nudge the body until it washed ashore and lay lifeless with the other debris while the rain drilled down unrelentingly. The con men would have written it with flourish and filmed it with style, and they had a fine day for the plying of their trades.

The men of the 87th Precinct weren't con men.

They only knew they had another floater.

The tattoo was obviously a mistake.

Mary Louise Proschek had had an almost identical tattoo. It had nestled snugly on the fold of skin between her right thumb and forefinger. The tattoo had been a heart, and the word *MAC* had decorated that heart. Mac—and a heart. A man—and love. For the con men throughout the ages have built a legend about the heart, have made the hardworking sump pump of the body the center of emotion, have disassociated love from the mind, have given a veneer of glamour to a bundle of muscle. It could have been worse. Their efforts could have descended upon the liver. In fact, the bile or the intestinal tract could have become the citadel of romance. The con men knew their trade. The shape of the heart makes a good symbol, easily recognized, easily worshipped. The eyes, the ears, the nose, the mind—the organs which see and hear and smell and know another human being, the organs which make another human being a living breathing part of yourself, a part as vital as your brain—these are discounted. St. Valentine had a good press agent.

The second floater was a girl.

There was a tattoo on the flap of skin between her right thumb and forefinger.

The tattoo was a heart.

There was a word in the heart.

And the word was *NAC.*

And, obviously, the tattoo was a mistake. Obviously, the man or woman who had been paid to decorate the skin had made a mistake. Obviously, he had been told to needle the word *MAC* into that heart, to fasten indelibly that man's name onto that girl's flesh. He had goofed. Perhaps he'd been drunk, or perhaps he'd been tired, or perhaps he simply didn't give a damn. Some people are that way, you know—no pride in their work. Whatever the case, the name had come out all wrong. Not a *MAC* this time, but a *NAC*. The man who'd thrown those girls into the water must have been absolutely furious. Nobody likes his byline misspelled.

The idea was to combine business with pleasure.

It was an idea Steve Carella didn't particularly relish, but he'd promised Teddy he'd meet her downtown at 8:00 on the button, and the call from the tattoo parlor had been clocked in at 7:45, and he knew it was too late to reach her at the house. He couldn't have called her, in any case, because the telephone was one instrument Carella's wife could never use. But he had, on other occasions, illegally dispatched a radio motor patrol car to his own apartment with the express purpose of delivering a message to Teddy. The police commissioner, even while allowing that Carella was a good cop, might have frowned upon such extracurricular squad car activity. So Carella, sneak that he was, never told him.

He stood now on the corner under the big bank clock, partially covered by the canopy that spread out over the entrance, shielding the big metal doors. He hoped there would not be an attempted bank robbery. If there was anything he disliked, it was foiling attempted bank robberies when he was off duty and waiting for the most beautiful woman in the world. Naturally, he was never off duty. A cop, as he well knew, is on duty 24 hours a day, 365 days a year, 366 days in leap year. Then, too, there was the tattoo parlor to visit, and he couldn't consider himself officially clocked out until he'd made that call and then reported the findings back to whoever was catching at the squad.

He hoped there would not be an attempted bank robbery, and he also hoped it would stop drizzling, because the rain was seeping into his bones and making his wounds ache. *Oh, my aching wounds!*

He put his aches out of his mind and fell to wool-gathering. Carella's favorite form of wool-gathering was thinking about his wife. He knew there was something hopelessly adolescent about the way he loved her, but those were the facts, ma'am, and there wasn't much he could do to change his feelings. There were probably more beautiful women in the world, but he didn't know who they were. There were probably sweeter, purer, warmer, more passionate women, too. He doubted it; he very strongly doubted it. The simple truth was that she pleased him. Hell, she delighted him. She had a face he would never tire of watching, a face that was a thousand faces, each linked subtly by a slender chain of beauty. Fully made up, her brown eyes glowing, the lashes darkened with mascara, her lips cleanly stamped with lipstick, she was one person—and he loved the meticulously calculated beauty, the freshly combed, freshly powdered veneer of that person.

In the morning, she was another person. Warm with sleep, her eyes would open, and her face would be undecorated, her full lips swollen, the black hair tangled like wild weeds, her body supple and pliable. He loved her this way, too, loved the small smile on her mouth and the sudden eager alertness of her eyes.

Her face was a thousand faces, quiet and introspective when they walked along a lonely shore barefoot and the only sound was the distant sound of breakers on the beach, a sound she could not hear in her silent world. Alive with fury, her face could change in an instant, the black brows swooping down over suddenly incandescent eyes, her lips skinning back over even, white teeth, her body taut with invective she could not hurl because she could not speak, her fists clenched. Tears transformed her face again. She did not cry often, and when she did cry, it was with completely unself-conscious anguish. It was almost as if, secure in the knowledge of her beauty, she could allow her face to be torn by agony.

Many men longed for the day when their ship would come in.

Carella's ship *had* come in—and it had launched a thousand faces.

There were times, of course, like *now*, when he wished the ship could do a little more than fifteen knots. It was 8:20, and she'd promised to be there at 8:00 on the dot, and whereas he never grew weary of her mental image, he much preferred her in person.

Now! For the first time! Live! On our stage! In person! Imported from the Cirque d'Hiver in Paris…

There must be something wrong with me, Carella thought. *I'm never really here. I'm always…*

He spotted her instantly. By this time, he was not surprised by what the sight of her could do to him. He had come to accept the instant quickening of his heart and the automatic smile on his face. She had not yet seen him, and he watched her from his secret vantage point, feeling somewhat sneaky, but what the hell!

She wore a black skirt and a red sweater and, over that, a black cardigan with red piping. The cardigan hung open, ending just below her hips. She had a feminine walk, which was completely unconscious, completely uncalculated. She walked rapidly because she was late, and he heard the steady clatter of the black pumps on the pavement, and he watched with delighted amusement the men who turned for a second look at his wife.

When she saw him, she broke into a run. He did not know what it was between them that made the shortest separation seem like a ten-year stretch at Alcatraz. Whatever it was, they had it. She came into his arms, and he kissed her soundly, and he wouldn't have given a damn if Twentieth Century Fox had been filming the entire sequence for a film titled *The Mating Season Jungle.*

"You're late," he said. "Don't apologize. You look lovely. We have to make a stop. Do you mind?"

Her eyes questioned his face.

"A tattoo parlor downtown. Guy thinks he may remember Mary Louise Proschek. We're lucky. This is business, so I was able to check out a sedan. Means we don't have to take the train home tonight. Some provider, your husband, huh?"

Teddy grinned and squeezed his arm.

"The car's around the corner. You look beautiful. You smell nice, too. What've you got on?"

Teddy dry-washed her hands.

"Just soap and water? You're amazing! Look how nice you can make soap smell. Honey, this won't take more than a few minutes. I've got some pictures of the Proschek girl in the car, and maybe we can get a make on them from this guy. After that, we'll eat and whatever you like. I can use a drink, can't you?"

Teddy nodded.

"Why do people always say they can 'use' a drink? What, when you get right down to it, can they 'use' it for?" He studied her and added, "I'm too talkative tonight. I guess I'm excited. We haven't had a night out in a long while. And you look beautiful. Don't you get tired of my saying that?"

Teddy shook her head, and there was a curious tenderness in the movement. He had grown used to her eyes, and perhaps he missed what they were saying to him, over and over again, repeatedly. Teddy Carella didn't need a tongue.

They walked to the car, and he opened the door for her, went around to the other side, and then started the motor. The police radio erupted into the closed sedan.

"*Car Twenty-one, Car Twenty-one, Signal One. Silvermine at North Fortieth...*"

"I'll be conscientious and leave it on," Carella said to Teddy. "Some pretty redhead may be trying to reach me."

Teddy's brows lowered menacingly.

"In connection with a case, of course," he explained.

Of course, she nodded mockingly.

"God, I love you," he said, his hand moving to her thigh. He squeezed her quickly, an almost unconscious gesture, and then he put his hand back on the wheel.

They drove steadily through the maze of city traffic. At one stoplight, a traffic cop yelled at Carella because he anticipated the changing of the light from red to green. The cop's raingear was slick with water. Carella felt suddenly like a heel.

The windshield wipers snicked at the steady drizzle. The tires whispered against the asphalt of the city. The city was locked in against the rain. People stood in doorways, leaned out of windows. There was a gray quietness to the city, as if the rain had suspended all activity, had caused the game of life to be called off. There was a rain smell to the city, too, all the smells of the day captured in the steady canopy of water and washed clean by it. There was, too, and strange for the city, a curious sense of peace.

"I love Paris when it drizzles," Carella said suddenly, and he did not have to explain the meaning of his words because she knew at once what he meant, she knew that he was not talking about Paris or Wichita, that he was talking about this city, his city, and that he had been born in it and into it, and that it, in turn, had been born into him.

The expensive apartment houses fell away behind them, as did the line of high-fashion stores, and the advertising agency towers, and the publishing shrines, and the gaudy brilliance of the amusement area, and the stilled emptiness of the garment district at night, and the tangled intricacy of the narrow side streets far downtown, the pushcarts filled with fruits and vegetables lining the streets, the store windows behind them, the Italian salami, and the provolone, and the pepperoni hanging in bright-red strings.

The tattoo parlor nestled in a side street on the fringe of Chinatown, straddled by a bar and a Laundromat. The combination of the three was somewhat absurd, ranging from the exotica of tattooing into the nether world of intoxication and from there to the plebeian task of laundering clothes. The neighborhood had seen its days of glory, perhaps, but they were all behind it. Far behind it. Like an old man with cancer, the neighborhood patiently and painfully awaited the end—and the end was the inevitable city housing project. And, in the meantime, nobody bothered to change the soiled bedclothes. Why bother when something was going to die anyway?

The man who ran the tattoo parlor was Chinese. The name on the plateglass window was Charlie Chen.

"Everybody call me Charlie Chan," he explained. "Big detective, Charlie Chan. But me *Chen*, Chen. You know Charlie Chan, Detective?"

"Yes," Carella said, smiling.

"Big detective," Chen said. "Got stupid sons." Chen laughed. "Me got stupid sons, too, but me no detective." He was a round, fat man, and everything he owned shook when he laughed. He had a small mustache on his upper lip, and he had thick fingers, and there was an oval jade ring on the forefinger of his left hand. "You detective, huh?" he asked.

"Yes," Carella said.

"This lady police lady?" Chen asked.

"No. This lady's my wife."

"Oh. Very good. Very good," Chen said. "Very pretty. She wants tattoo, maybe? Do nice butterfly for her on shoulder. Very good for strapless gowns. Very pretty. Very decorative."

Teddy shook her head, smiling.

"Very pretty lady. You very lucky detective," Chen said. He turned to Teddy. "Nice yellow butterfly, maybe? Very pretty?" He opened his eyes seductively. "Everybody say very pretty."

Teddy shook her head again.

"Maybe you like red better? Red your color, maybe? Nice red butterfly?"

Teddy could not keep herself from smiling. She kept shaking her head and smiling, feeling very much a part of her husband's work, happy that he'd had to make the call and happy that he'd taken her with him. It was curious, she supposed, but she did not know him as a cop. His function as a cop was something almost completely alien to her, even though he talked about his work. She knew that he dealt with crime, and the perpetrators of crime, and she often wondered what kind of man he was when he was on the job. Heartless? She could not imagine that in her man. Cruel? No. Hard? Tough? Perhaps.

"About this girl," Carella said to Chen. "When did she come in for the tattoo?"

"Oh, long time ago," Chen said. "Maybe five months, maybe six. Nice lady. Not so pretty like your lady, but very nice."

"Was she alone?"

"No. She with tall man." Chen scrutinized Carella's face. "Prettier than you, Detective."

Carella grinned. "What did he look like?"

"Tall. Movie star. Very handsome. Muscles."

"What color was his hair?"

"Yellow," Chen said.

"His eyes?"

Chen shrugged.

"Anything you remember about him?"

"He smile all the time," Chen said. "Big white teeth. Very pretty teeth. Very handsome man. Movie star."

"Tell me what happened?"

"They come in together. She hold his arm. She look at him, stars in her eyes." Chen paused. "Like your lady. But not so pretty."

"Were they married?"

Chen shrugged.

"Did you see an engagement ring or a wedding band on her finger?"

"I don't see," Chen said. He grinned at Teddy. Teddy grinned back. "You like black butterfly? Pretty black wings? Come, I show you." He led them into the shop. A beaded curtain led to the back room. The walls of the shop were covered with tattoo designs. A calendar with a nude girl on it hung on the wall near the beaded curtain. Someone had jokingly inked tattoos onto her entire body. The tattooer had drawn a pair of clutching hands on the girl's full breasts. Chen pointed to a butterfly design on one of the walls.

"This butterfly. You like? You pick color. Any color. I do. I put on your shoulder. Very pretty."

"Tell me what happened with the girl," Carella said, gently insistent.

Teddy looked at him curiously. Her husband was enjoying the byplay between herself and Chen, but he was not losing sight of his objective. He was here in this shop for a possible lead on the man who had killed Mary Louise Proschek. She suddenly felt that if the byplay got too involved, her husband would call a screaming halt to it.

"They come in shop. He say the girl want tattoo. I show them designs on wall. I try to sell her butterfly. Nobody like butterfly. Butterfly my own design. Very pretty. Good for shoulder. I do butterfly on one lady's back, near base of spine. Very pretty, only nobody see. Good for shoulder. I try to sell her butterfly, but man say he wants heart. She say she wants heart, too. Stars in eyes, you know? Big love, big thing, shining all over. I show them big hearts. Very pretty hearts, very complicated, many colors."

"They didn't want a big heart?"

"Man wants small heart. He show me where." Chen spread his thumb and forefinger. "Here. Very difficult. Skinny flesh, needle could go through. Very painful. Very difficult. He say he wants it there. Say if he wants it there, she wants it there. Crazy."

"Who suggested what lettering to put into the heart?"

"Man. He say, 'You put M-A-C in heart.'"

"He said to put the name *Mac* into that heart?"

"He no say name *Mac*. He say put M-A-C."

"And what did she say?"

"She say, 'Yes, M-A-C.'"

"Go on."

"I do. Very painful. Girl scream. He hold her shoulders. Very painful. Tender spot." Chen shrugged. "Butterfly on shoulder better."

"Did she mention his name while she was here?"

"No."

"Did she call him Mac?"

"She call him nothing." Chen thought a moment. "Yes, she call him darling, dear, sweetheart. Love words. No name."

Carella sighed. He lifted the flap of the manila envelope in his hands and drew out the glossy prints that were inside it. "Is this the girl?" he asked Chen.

Chen looked at the pictures. "That she," he said. "She dead, huh?"

"Yes, she's dead."

"He kill her?"

"We don't know."

"She love him," Chen said, wagging his head. "Love very special. Nobody should kill love."

Teddy looked at the little round Chinese, and she suddenly felt very much like allowing him to tattoo his prize butterfly design on her shoulder. Carella took the pictures back and put them into the envelope.

"Has this man ever come into your shop again?" Carella asked. "With another woman, perhaps?"

"No, never," Chen said.

"Well," Carella said, "thanks a lot, Mr. Chen. If you remember anything more about him, give me a call, won't you?" He opened his wallet. "Here's my card. Just ask for Detective Carella."

"You come back," Chen said. "You ask for Charlie Chan, big detective, with stupid sons. You bring wife. I make pretty butterfly on shoulder." He extended his hand, and Carella took it. For a moment, Chen's eyes went serious. "You lucky," he said. "You not so pretty, have very pretty lady. Love very special." He turned to Teddy. "Someday, if you want butterfly, you come back. I make very pretty." He winked. "Detective husband like. I promise. Any color. Ask for Charlie Chan. That's me."

He grinned and wagged his head, and Carella and Teddy left the shop, heading for the police sedan up the street.

"Nice guy, wasn't he?" Carella said.

Teddy nodded.

"I wish they were all like him. A lot of them aren't. With many people, the presence of a cop automatically produces a feeling of guilt. That's the truth, Teddy. They instantly feel that they're under suspicion, and everything they say becomes defensive. I guess that's because there are skeletons in the cleanest closets. Are you very hungry?"

Teddy made a face that indicated she was famished.

"Shall we find a place in the neighborhood, or do you want to wait until we get uptown?"

Teddy pointed to the ground.

"Here?"

Yes, she nodded.

"Chinese?"

No.

"Italian?"

Yes.

"You shouldn't have married a guy of Italian descent," Carella said. "Whenever such a guy eats in an Italian restaurant, he can't help comparing his spaghetti with what his mother used to cook. He then becomes dissatisfied with what he's eating, and the dissatisfaction spreads to include his wife. The next thing you know, he's suing for divorce."

Teddy put her forefingers to her eyes, stretching the skin so that her eyes became slitted.

"Right," Carella said. "You should have married a Chinese. But then, of course, you wouldn't be able to eat in Chinese restaurants." He paused and grinned. "All this eating talk is making me hungry. How about that place up the street?"

They walked to it rapidly, and Carella looked through the plateglass window.

"Not too crowded," he said, "and it looks clean. You game?"

Teddy took his arm, and he led her into the place.

It was, perhaps, not the cleanest place in the world. As sharp as Carella's eyes were, a cursory glance through a plateglass window is not always a good evaluation of cleanliness. And, perhaps, the reason it wasn't too crowded was that the food wasn't too good. Not that it mattered very much, since both Carella and Teddy were really very hungry and probably would have eaten sautéed grasshoppers if they were served.

The place did have nice checkered tablecloths and candles stuck into the necks of old wine bottles, the wax frozen to the glass. The place did have a long bar, which ran the length of the wall opposite the dining room, bottles stacked behind it, amber lights illuminating the bottles. The place did have a phone booth, and Carella still had to make his call back to the squad.

The waiter who came over to their table seemed happy to see them.

"Something to drink before you order?" he asked.

"Two martinis," Carella said. "Olives."

"Would you care to see a menu now or later, sir?"

"Might as well look at it now," Carella said. The waiter brought them two menus. Carella glanced at his briefly and then put it down. "I'm bucking for a divorce," he said. "I'll have spaghetti."

While Teddy scanned the menu, Carella looked around the room. An elderly couple was quietly eating at a table near the phone booth. There was no one else in the dining room. At the bar, a man in a leather jacket sat with a shot glass and a glass of water before him. The man was looking into the bar mirror. His eyes were on Teddy. Behind the bar, the bartender was mixing the martinis Carella had ordered.

"I'm so damn hungry I could eat the bartender," Carella said.

When the waiter came with their drinks, he ordered spaghetti for himself and then asked Teddy what she wanted. Teddy pointed to the lasagna dish on the menu, and Carella gave it to the waiter. When the waiter was gone, they picked up their glasses.

"Here's to ships that come in," Carella said.

Teddy stared at him, puzzled.

"All loaded with treasures from the east," he went on, "smelling of rich spices, with golden sails."

She was still staring at him, still puzzled.

"I'm drinking to you, darling," he explained. He watched the smile form on her mouth. "Poetic cops this city can do without," he said, and he sipped at the martini and then put the glass down. "I want to call the squad, honey. I'll be back in a minute." He touched her hand briefly and then went toward the phone booth, digging in his pocket for change as he walked away from the table.

She watched him walk from her, pleased with the long athletic strides he took, pleased with the impatience of his hand as it dug for change, pleased with the way he held his head. She realized abruptly that one of the first things that had attracted her to Carella was the way he moved. There was an economy and simplicity of motion about him, a sense of directness. You got the feeling that before he moved he knew exactly where he was going and what he was going to do, and so there was a tremendous sense of security attached to being with him.

Teddy sipped at the martini and then took a long swallow. She had not eaten since noon, and so she was not surprised by the rapidity with which the martini worked its alcoholic wonders. She watched her husband enter the phone booth, watched as he dialed quickly. She wondered how he would speak to the desk sergeant and then to the detective who was catching in the squadroom. *Would they know he'd been talking of treasure ships just a few moments before? What kind of a cop was he? What did the other cops think of him?* She felt a sudden exclusion. Faced with the impenetrable privacy that was any man's work, she felt alone and unwanted. Quickly, she drained the martini glass.

A shadow fell over the table.

At first she thought it was only a trick of her eyes, and then she looked up. The man who'd been sitting at the bar, the man in the leather jacket, was standing at the table, grinning.

"Hi," he said.

She glanced hastily at the phone booth. Carella had his back to the dining room.

"What're you doing with a creep like that?" the man said.

Teddy turned away from him and fastened her eyes to the napkin in her lap.

"You're just about the cutest doll that ever walked into this dump," the man in the leather jacket said. "Why don't you ditch that creep and meet me later. How about it?"

She could smell whiskey on the man's breath. There was something frightening about his eyes, something insulting about the way they roamed her body with open candor. She wished she were not wearing a sweater. Unconsciously, she pulled the cardigan closed over the jutting cones of her breasts.

"Come on," the man said, "don't cover them up."

She looked up at him and shook her head. Her eyes pleaded with him to go away. She glanced again to the phone booth. Carella was talking animatedly.

"My name's Dave," the man said. "That's a nice name, ain't it? Dave. What's your name?"

She could not answer him. She would not have answered him even if she could.

"Come on, loosen up," Dave said. He stared at her, and his eyes changed, and he said, "Jesus, you're beautiful, you know that? Ditch him, will you? Ditch him and meet me."

Teddy shook her head.

"Let me hear you talk," Dave said.

She shook her head again, pleadingly this time.

"I want to hear your voice. I'll bet it's the sexiest goddamn voice in the world. Let me hear it."

Teddy squeezed her eyes shut tightly. Her hands were trembling in her lap. She wanted this man to go away, wanted him to leave her alone, wanted him to be gone before Steve came out of that booth, before Steve came back to the table. She was slightly dizzy from the martini, and her mind could only think that Steve would be displeased, that Steve might think she had invited this.

"Look, what do you have to be such a cold tomato for, huh? I'll bet you're not so cold. I'll bet you're pretty warm. Let me hear your voice."

She shook her head again, and then she saw Carella hang up the phone and open the door of the booth. He was grinning, and then he looked toward the table and the grin dropped from his mouth, and she felt a sudden sick panic at the pit of her stomach. Carella moved out of the booth quickly. His eyes had tightened into focus on the man with the leather jacket.

"Come on," Dave said, "what you got to be that way for, huh? All I'm asking—"

"What's the trouble, mister?" Carella said suddenly. She looked up at her husband, wanting him to know she had not asked for this, hoping it was in her eyes. Carella did not turn to look at her. His eyes were riveted to Dave's face.

"No trouble at all," Dave said, turning to face Carella with an arrogant smile.

"You're annoying my wife," Carella said. "Take off."

"Oh, was I annoying her? Is the little lady your wife?" He spread his legs wide and let his arms dangle at his sides, and Carella knew instantly that he was looking for trouble and wouldn't be happy until he found it.

"You were, and she is," Carella said. "Go crawl back to the bar. It's been nice knowing you."

Dave continued smiling. "I ain't crawling back nowhere," he said. "This is a free country. I'm staying right here."

Carella shrugged and pulled out his chair. Dave continued standing by the table. Carella took Teddy's hand.

"Are you all right?" he asked.

Teddy nodded.

"Ain't that sweet?" Dave said. "Big handsome hubby comes back from—"

Carella dropped his wife's hand and stood suddenly. At the other end of the dining room, the elderly couple looked up from their meal.

"Mister," Carella said slowly, "you're bothering the hell out of me. You'd better—"

"Am I bothering you?" Dave said. "Hell, all I'm doing is admiring a nice piece of—" and Carella hit him.

He hit him suddenly, with the full force of his arm and shoulder behind the blow. He hit him suddenly and full in the mouth, and Dave staggered back from the table and slammed into the next table, knocking the wine bottle candle to the floor. He leaned on the table for a moment, and when he looked up, his mouth was bleeding, but he was still smiling.

"I was hoping you'd do that, pal," he said. He studied Carella for a moment, and then he lunged at him.

Teddy sat with her hands clenched in her lap, her face white. She saw her husband's face, and it was not the face of the man she knew and loved. The face was completely expressionless, the mouth a hard, tight line that slashed it horizontally, the eyes narrowed so that the pupils were barely visible, the nostrils wide and flaring. He stood spread-legged with his fists balled, and she looked at his hands, and they seemed bigger than they'd ever seemed before, big and powerful, lethal weapons that hung at his sides, waiting. His entire body seemed to be waiting. She could feel the coiled-spring tautness of him as he waited for Dave's rush, and he seemed like a smoothly functioning, well-oiled machine in that moment, a machine which would react automatically as soon as the right button were pushed, as soon as the right lever were pressed. There was nothing human about the machine. All humanity had left Steve Carella the moment his fist had lashed out at Dave. What Teddy saw now was a highly trained and a highly skilled technician about to do his work, waiting for the response buttons to be pushed.

Dave did not know he was fighting a machine. Ignorantly, he pushed out at the buttons.

Carella's left fist hit him in the gut, and he doubled over in pain, and then Carella threw a flashing uppercut, which caught

Dave under the chin and sent him sprawling backward against the table again. Carella moved quickly and effortlessly, like a cue ball under the hands of an expert pool player, sinking one ball and then rolling to position for a good shot at the next ball. Before Dave clambered off the table, Carella was in position again, waiting.

When Teddy saw Dave pick up the wine bottle, her mouth opened in shocked anguish. But she knew somehow this did not come as a surprise to her husband. His eyes, his face, did not change. He watched dispassionately while Dave hit the bottle against the table. The jagged shards of the bottleneck clutched in Dave's fist frightened her until she wanted to scream, until she wished she had a voice so that she could scream until her throat ached. She knew her husband would be cut, she knew that Dave was drunk enough to cut him, and she watched Dave advancing with the broken bottle, but Carella did not budge an inch. He stood there motionless, his body balanced on the balls of his feet, his right hand open, the fingers widespread, his left hand flat and stiff at his side.

Dave lunged with the broken bottle. He passed low, aiming for Carella's groin. A look of surprise crossed his face when he felt Carella's right hand clamp onto his wrist. He felt himself falling forward suddenly, pulled by Carella who had stepped back lightly on his right foot, and who was raising his left hand high over his head, the hand still stiff and rigid.

And then Carella's left hand descended. Hard and straight, like the sharp biting edge of an ax, it moved downward with remarkable swiftness. Dave felt the impact of the blow. The hard, calloused edge of Carella's hand struck him on the side of his neck, and then Dave bellowed and Carella swung his left hand across his own body, and again, the hand fell, this time on the opposite side of Dave's neck, and he fell to the floor, both arms paralyzed for the moment, unable to move.

Carella stood over him, waiting.

"Lay...lay off," Dave said.

The waiter stood at the entrance to the dining room, his eyes wide.

"Get the police," Carella said, his voice curiously toneless.

"But—" the waiter started.

"I'm a detective," Carella said. "Get the patrolman on the beat. Hurry up!"

"Yes," the waiter said. "Yes, sir."

Carella did not move from where he stood over Dave. He did not once look at Teddy. When the patrolman arrived, he showed his shield and told him to book Dave for disorderly conduct, generously neglecting to mention assault. He gave the patrolman all the information he needed, walked out with him to the squad car, and was gone for some five minutes. When he came back to the table, the elderly couple had gone. Teddy sat staring at her napkin.

"Hi," he said, and he grinned.

She looked across the table at him.

"I'm sorry," he said. "I didn't want trouble."

She shook her head.

"He'll be better off locked up for the night. He'd only have picked on someone else, hon. He was spoiling for a fight." He paused. "The next guy he might have succeeded in cutting."

Teddy Carella nodded and sighed heavily. She had just had a visit to her husband's office and seen him at work. And she could still remember the terrible swiftness of his hands, hands which she had only known tenderly before.

And so she sighed heavily because she had just discovered the world was not populated with gentle little boys playing games.

And then she reached across the table, and she took his right hand and brought it to her mouth, and she kissed the knuckles, and she kissed the palm, and Carella was surprised to feel the wetness of her tears against his flesh.

It was unfortunate, perhaps, that Arthur Brown was so zealous in his pursuit of the con man. Had he not been such an eager beaver, he would not have asked to replace Carella when Carella drew Lineup that week. Lineup means a trip downtown to Headquarters on High Street, and Lineup means sitting in a room with a pile of other detectives from all over the city, watching the parade of felony offenders. Lineup is sometimes exciting; usually, it's a bore.

Brown, as it happened, had just held his personal lineup in the squadroom of the 87th Precinct, whereat he paraded Frederick "Fritzie" Deutsch before a little Negro girl named Betty Prescott and a big businessman named Elliot Jamison. Both victims had cleared Deutsch at once. He was not the man (or in Jamison's case, *either* of the men) who had conned them. Brown was secretly pleased. He had thanked both Miss Prescott and Mr.

Jamison and then clapped Deutsch on the back and gruffly said, "Keep your nose clean."

And then he had asked Carella if he could take his place at the lineup the next day. Carella, who considered the lineup a necessary evil—something like a mother-in-law who comes to live with you—readily relinquished the duty. Had Carella been the sort of cop who loved Lineup, had Carella been more conscientious, more devoted to detail, had Carella felt any real purpose would be served by his appearance at Headquarters that Wednesday, things might have worked out differently.

Actually, Carella *was* conscientious, and he *was* devoted to detail—but he was up to his ears in floaters and the lineup very rarely turned up any good murder suspects. His time, he assumed, could be better spent in a thorough rundown of the city's tattoo parlors in an effort to track down the *NAC* that had appeared on the second floater's hand.

So he allowed Brown to take his place, and that was most unfortunate.

It was unfortunate in that there were two handsome blond men who were shown at the lineup that Wednesday.

One of them had killed Mary Louise Proschek and the second unidentified floater.

Brown was interested, at the moment, in con men—not murderers.

Carella was interested in tattoo parlors.

Kling was a new cop.

He accompanied Brown to Headquarters on that Wednesday. The city was, again, blanketed with a dreary drizzle, and the men spoke very little on the long ride downtown. Kling, for the most part, was thinking of breaking his vacation date to Claire and wondering how she would react to it. Brown was thinking about his con man, who had acted singly once and in concert a second time, and wondering if the lineup would turn up anything. Brown drove slowly because of the slick pavement. They did not reach Headquarters until 9:05. By the time the elevator had taken them to the ninth floor, the lineup had been underway for some ten minutes. They pinned their shields to their jackets and passed through the patrolman outside at the desk in the corridor. The patrolman said nothing. He simply looked at his watch condemningly.

The large gymnasium-like room was dark when they entered it. The only area of light was at the far end of the room, where the stage was brilliantly illuminated.

"...third stickup in 1949," the chief of detectives said from his dais behind the rows and rows of folding chairs upon which detectives from every precinct in the city sat. "Thought we'd cured you that time, Alphonse, but apparently, you never learn. Now how about that gas station last night?"

The man on the stage was silent. The microphone hung before his face on a solid steel pipe, and the graduated height markers on the wall behind him told the assembled bulls that he was five foot eight.

Kling and Brown made their way unobtrusively past the dais and speaking stand and then shuffled into one of the rows, sitting as quickly and quietly as they could.

"I'm talking to you, Alphonse," the chief of detectives said. "Never mind the latecomers," he added sarcastically, and Kling felt a hot flush spread over his face.

"I hear you fine," Alphonse said.

"Then how about it?"

"I don't have to say nothing at a lineup, and you know it."

"You've been to a lot of lineups, huh?"

"A couple."

"On these other stickups?"

"Yeah."

"Never thought you'd be here again on a stickup, did you?"

"I got nothing to say," Alphonse said. "You got to prove there was a stickup and that I done it."

"That shouldn't be too hard," the chief of detectives said. "It might go a little easier on you if you told us what we wanted to know, though."

"Snow jobs I can do without so early in the morning," Alphonse said. "I know the setup. Don't ask questions, 'cause I know I don't have to answer them."

"All right," the chief of detectives conceded. "Next case."

Alphonse walked off the stage, his movements followed by every eye in the room. For the purpose of these Monday-to-Thursday, early-morning parades was simply to acquaint every detective in the city with the men who were committing crime in their city. Sometimes, a victim was invited to the lineup in an attempt to identify a suspect, but such occasions were rare and usually fruitless. They were rare because a victim generally had a thousand good reasons for not wanting to be at the lineup. They were usually fruitless because a victim generally had a thousand good reasons for not wanting to identify a suspect. The least valid of these reasons, if the most popularly accepted, was fear of reprisal. In any case, not many suspects were identified by victims. Were this the sole purpose of the lineup, the whole affair would have been a dreadful flop. On the other hand, the bulls who congregated at headquarters every Monday-to-Thursday morning—as much as they disliked the task—studied the felony offenders of the day before with close scrutiny. You never knew when you'd get a lead to the case you were working on. And you never knew when it might be important to recognize a cheap thief on the street. Such recognition might, in rare cases, even save your life.

And so the chief of detectives went through the prescribed ritual, and the bulls listened and watched.

"Riverhead, one," the chief of detectives said, calling off the area of the city in which the arrest had been made and the number of the case from that area that day. "Riverhead, one. Hunter, Curt, thirty-five. Drinking heavily in a bar on Shelter Place. Got into an argument with the bartender and hurled a chair at the bar mirror. No statement. What happened, Curt?"

Hunter had been led to the steps at the side of the stage by his arresting officer, a burly patrolman. The patrolman would have had to be burly to arrest Hunter, who cleared the six-foot-two marker and who must have weighed about 200 pounds. He had broad shoulders and a narrow waist, and he took aggressive strides to where the microphone hung. He had blond hair, combed slickly back from a wide forehead. He had a straight nose and steel-gray eyes. His cheekbones were high, and his mouth was a strong mouth, and his chin was cleft. He looked as if he were walking on stage to take instructions from a director rather than to face the fire of the chief of detectives.

"How about what?" he asked.

"What'd you argue about?" the chief of detectives said.

Hunter crowded the microphone. "That jail I was in last night was a pigsty. Somebody puked all over the floor."

"We're not here to discuss—"

"I'm no goddamn criminal!" Hunter shouted. "I got into a little fray, all right. That's no reason to put me in a cell smelling of somebody's goddamn vomit!"

"You should have thought of that before you committed a felony," the chief of detectives said.

"Felony?" Hunter shouted. "Is getting drunk a felony?"

"No, but assault is. You hit that bartender, didn't you?"

"All right, I hit him," Hunter said.

"That's assault."

"I didn't hit him with anything but my fist!"

"That's second-degree assault."

"There are guys hitting guys every day of the week," Hunter said. "I don't see them getting pulled in on first-degree or second-degree or even third-degree assault."

"This is your first offense, isn't it?" the chief of detectives asked.

"Yeah, yeah," Hunter said.

"Relax, you may get off with just a fine. Now, let's hear the story."

"The bartender called me 'pretty boy,'" Hunter said.

"So you hit him?"

"No, not then. I hit him later."

"Why?"

"He said something about us big handsome hunks of men never being any good with a woman. He said you could never judge a book by its cover. That's when I hit him."

"Why'd you throw the chair at the bar mirror?"

"Well, I hit him, and he called me a name."

"What name?"

"A name."

"We've heard them all," the chief of detectives said. "Let's have it."

"It's a name I associate with abnormal men," Hunter said. "That's when I threw the chair. I wasn't aiming at the mirror; I was aiming at him. That son of a bitch! I can get any woman I want!"

"You always lose your temper so easily?" the chief of detectives asked.

"Not usually," Hunter said.

"What made you so touchy last night?"

"I was just touchy," Hunter said.

"The arresting officer found a thousand dollars in small bills in your pocket. How about that?"

"Yeah, how about that?" Hunter shouted. "When do I get it back? I hit a guy, and next thing you know, I'm being robbed and thrown into a cell that smells of vomit."

"Where'd you get that thousand?"

"From the bank," Hunter said.

"Which bank?"

"My bank. The bank where I save."

"When did you withdraw it?"

"Yesterday afternoon."

"Why?"

Hunter hesitated.

"Well?"

"I thought I might take a little trip," Hunter said. His voice had become suddenly subdued. He squinted into the lights, as if trying to read the face of his questioner.

"What kind of a trip?"

"Pleasure."

"Where?"

"Upstate."

"Alone?"

Hunter hesitated again.

"How about it, Curt? Alone or with somebody?"

"With somebody," Hunter said.

"Who?"

"A girl."

"*Who?*"

"That's my business."

"That's your pleasure," the chief of detectives corrected, and all the bulls—including Brown and Kling—laughed. "What happened to change your plans?"

"Nothing," Hunter said, annoyed by the laughter, on guard now, waiting for the next question.

"You drew a thousand dollars from your bank yesterday afternoon, is that right?"

"Yes."

"Because you thought you just *might* take a little trip with a girl. Last night, you're drinking alone in a bar, the thousand dollars in your pocket, and a bartender says something about your inability to please a woman, so you haul off and sock him. Is that right?"

"Yes, that's right."

"Okay. What happened? The girl call it off?"

"That's my business," Hunter said again.

"Do you like girls?" the chief of detectives asked.

Hunter's eyes were narrow now, peering into the lights suspiciously. "Don't *you*?" he asked.

"I love 'em," the chief of detectives said. "But I'm asking you."

"I like 'em fine," Hunter said.

"This girl you planned the trip with—a special friend?"

"A doll," Hunter said, his face blank.

"But a friend?"

"A doll," he repeated, and the chief of detectives knew that was all he'd get from Hunter. The tall, handsome blond man waited.

Kling watched him, never once connecting him with the blond man who had allegedly led Mary Louise Proschek into Charlie Chen's tattoo parlor. Kling had read Carella's report, but his mind simply did not make any connection.

"Next case," the chief of detectives said, and Hunter walked across the stage.

When he reached the steps on the other side, he turned and shouted, "The city hasn't heard the end of that goddamn pukey prison!" and then he went down the steps.

"Riverhead, two," the chief of detectives said. "Donaldson, Chris, thirty-five. Tried to pick a man's pocket in the subway. Transit cop made the pinch. Donaldson stated it was a mistake. How about it, Chris?"

Chris Donaldson could have been a double for Curt Hunter. As he walked across the stage, in fact, the chief of detectives murmured, "What is this? A twin act?" Donaldson was tall and blond and handsome. If there were any detectives in the audience with inferiority complexes, the combination of Hunter and Donaldson should have been enough to shove them over the thin line to psychosis. It was doubtful that the lineup had ever had such a combined display of masculine splendor since its inception. Donaldson seemed as unruffled as Hunter had been. He walked to the microphone. His head crossed the six-foot-three marker on the white wall behind him.

"There's been a mistake," Donaldson said.

"Really?"

"Yes," he said calmly. "I didn't pick anybody's pocket, nor did I attempt to. I'm a gainfully employed citizen. The man whose pocket was picked simply accused the wrong person."

"Then how come we found his wallet in your jacket pocket?"

"I have no idea," Donaldson said. "Unless the real pickpocket dropped it there when he felt he was about to be discovered."

"Tell us what happened," the chief of detectives said, and then in an aside to the assembled bulls, he added, "This man has no record."

"I was riding the subway home from work," Donaldson said. "I work in Isola, live in Riverhead. I was reading my newspaper. The man standing in front of me suddenly wheeled around and said, 'Where's my wallet? Somebody took my wallet!'"

"Then what?"

"The car was packed. A man standing alongside us said he was a transit cop, and before you knew it, another man and I were grabbed and held. The cop searched us and found the wallet in my pocket."

"Where'd the other man go?"

"I have no idea. When the transit cop found the wallet on me, he lost all interest in the other man."

"And your story is that the other man was the pickpocket."

"I don't know who the pickpocket was. I only know that he wasn't me. As I told you, I *work* for a living."

"What do you do?"

"I'm an accountant."

"For whom?"

"Binks and Lederle. It's one of the oldest accounting firms in the city. I've worked there for a good many years."

"Well, Chris," the chief of detectives said, "it sounds good. It's up to the judge, though."

"There are people, you know," Donaldson said, "who sue the city for false arrest."

"We don't know if it's false arrest yet, do we?"

"*I'm* quite sure of it," Donaldson said. "I've led an honest life, and I have no desire to get involved with the police."

"Nobody does," the chief of detectives said. "Next case."

Donaldson walked off the stage. Kling watched him, wondering if his story were true, again making no connection between Mary Louise Proschek's blond escort and the man who'd claimed he'd been falsely accused of pickpocketing.

"Diamondback, one," the chief of detectives said. "Pereira, Genevieve, forty-seven. Slashed her husband with a bread knife. No statement. What happened, Jenny?"

Genevieve Pereira was a short woman with shrewd blue eyes. She stood with her lips pursed and her hands clasped. She was dressed neatly and quietly, the only garish thing about her being a smear of blood across the front of her dress.

"I detect an error in your notations, sir," she said.

"Do you?"

"You've misrepresented me chronologically by two years. My age is only forty-five."

"Forgive me, Jenny," the chief of detectives said.

"I feel, too, that your familiarity is somewhat uncalled-for. Only my closest acquaintances call me Jenny. The appellation, for your exclusive benefit, is Genevieve."

"Thank you," the chief of detectives said, a smile in his voice. "And may I call you that?"

"If the necessity is so overwhelming," Genevieve said.

"Why'd you stab your husband, Genevieve?"

"I did not stab him," Genevieve answered. "He suffered, at best, a surface scratch. I'm sure he'll convalesce."

"You speak English beautifully," the chief of detectives said.

"Your praise, though unsolicited," Genevieve said, "is nonetheless appreciated. I've always tried to avoid dull clichés and transparent repetition."

"Well, it certainly comes out beautifully," the chief of detectives said, and Kling detected a new note of sarcasm.

"Any perseverant person can master the English tongue," Genevieve said. "Application is all that is required. Plus, an abundant amount of native intelligence. And a detestation of the obvious."

"Like what?"

"I'm sure I could not readily produce any examples." She paused. "I would have to cogitate on it momentarily. I suggest, instead, that you read some of the various works of literature that have aided me."

"Books like what?" the chief of detectives asked, and this time the sarcasm was unmistakable. "*English for Martians*? Or *The English Language As A Lethal Weapon*?"

"I find sarcastic males vulgar," Genevieve said.

"Did you find stabbing your husband vulgar?"

"I did not stab him. I scratched him with a knife. I see no reason for promoting this case to federal proportions."

"Why'd you stab him?"

"Nor do I see," Genevieve persisted, "any pertinent reasons for discussing my marital affairs before an assemblage of barbarians." She paused and cleared her throat. "If you would relinquish my wrapper, I assure you I would depart without—"

"Sure," the chief of detectives said. "Next case."

And that's the way it went.

When it was all over, Kling and Brown went downstairs and lighted cigarettes.

"No con man," Brown said.

"These lineups are a waste of time," Kling offered. He blew out a stream of smoke. "How'd you like those two handsome bastards?"

Brown shrugged. "Come on," he said, "we better get back to the squad."

The two handsome bastards, considering the fact that one of them was a murderer, got off pretty lightly.

Curt Hunter was found guilty and paid a $500 fine, plus damages.

Chris Donaldson was found not guilty.

Both men were, once again, free to roam the city.

Bert Kling expected trouble, and he was getting it.

Usually, he and Claire Townsend got along just jim-dandy. They'd had their quarrels, true, but who was there to claim that the path of true love ever ran smooth? In fact, considering the bad start their romance had had, their love was chugging along on a remarkably even keel. Kling had had a rough time in the beginning trying to dislodge the torch Claire was carrying from the firm grip with which she'd carried it. He'd succeeded. They had passed through the getting-acquainted stages, and had then progressed rapidly through the con man's legend of going steady, and then through the con man's formality of getting engaged, and then—if they weren't careful—they would enter the con man's legality of getting married, and then the con man's nightmare of having children.

Provided they could leap this particular hurdle that confronted them on that Wednesday night.

The hurdle was a very high one.

Kling was learning, perhaps a little late to do anything about it, that hell hath no fury like a woman scorned.

The woman scorned was rather tall by American standards. Not too tall for Kling, but she'd have given the run-of-the-mill, unheroic American male trouble unless she wore flats on her dates. The woman scorned had black hair cut close to her head and brown eyes, which were aglow now with an inner fury, and a good mouth, which was twisted into a somewhat sardonic grin. The woman scorned was slender without being skinny, bosomy without being busty, leggy without being gangly. The woman scorned was, as a matter of fact, damned pretty even when she was venting her fury.

"You *know*," she said, "that this probably means no vacation, don't you?"

"I don't know that at all," Kling said. "I have no reason to believe that."

"You are not, if you'll pardon my pointing it out, writing up a traffic ticket at the moment."

"Nor did I intend to sound as if I were," Kling said, amazed by the high level of their argument, thinking at the same time that Claire looked quite lovely when she was angry and wanting simultaneously to kiss the fury off her mouth.

"I realize that the 87th Precinct is just *loaded* with super masterminds who have all sorts of priority over a dumb rookie who just got promoted. But, for God's sake, Bert—"

"Claire—"

"You *did* crack a murder case, you know! And the commissioner *did* personally commend you and *did* personally promote you! What do you have to do in order to get a vacation spot that jibes with your fiancée's schedule? Stop mass fratricide? Cure the common cold?"

"Claire, it's not a question of—"

"Whatever you have to do, you should have *done* it!" Claire snapped. "Of all the idiotic times for a vacation, June tenth absolutely takes the brass bologna! Of all the incredibly ridiculous—"

"It's not my fault, Claire. Claire, the schedule is made out by Lieutenant—"

"…incredibly ridiculous times for a vacation, June tenth positively wins the fur-lined bathtub!"

"All right," Kling said.

"All right?" she repeated. "What's all right about it? It reeks! It's bureaucracy in action! Hell, it's totalitarianism!"

"It's a hell of a thing, all right," Kling agreed. "Would you like me to quit my job? Shall I get a nice democratic position like shoemaker or butcher or—"

"Oh, stop it."

"If I were a midget," Kling said, "I could probably get a job stuffing Vienna sausages. Trouble is—"

"Stop it," she said again, but she was smiling.

"You better?" he asked hopefully.

"I'm sick," she answered.

"It's a tough break."

"Let's have a drink."

"Rye neat," he said.

Claire looked at him. "No need to go all to pieces, Officer," she said. "It's not the end of the world. Worst comes to worst, you can go on vacation with some other girl."

"That sounds like a good idea," Kling said, snapping his fingers.

"And all I'll do is break both your arms," Claire said. She poured two hookers of rye and handed one of them to Kling. "Here's to a solution."

"You just hit the solution," Kling said, raising the glass to his lips. "Another girl."

"Don't you dare drink to that!" Claire said.

"You're sure finals don't begin until the seventeenth?"

"Positive."

"Can you swing something?"

"Like what?"

"I don't know." Kling looked into the eye of his glass. "Aw, hell," he said, "here's to a solution," and he threw it down.

Claire swallowed hers without batting an eyelid. "Let's think," she said.

"How many tests are there?" Kling asked.

"Five," she answered.

"When is school over?"

"Classes end on the seventh of June. The next week is a reading week. And then finals start on the seventeenth."

"When do they end?"

"Two weeks later. That's when the semester is officially over."

"June twenty-eighth?"

"Yes."

"That's great. I need another drink."

"No more. We need clear heads."

"How about you taking your tests during that last week of classes?"

"Impossible."

"Why?"

"I don't know. It just is."

"Has it ever been done before?"

"I doubt it strongly."

"Hell, this is an emergency."

"Is it? Bert, Women's U is an all-girls school. Can I go to the dean and say I'd like to have permission to take my finals the week of the third because my boyfriend and I are leaving on vacation the following week?"

"Why not?"

"They'd probably expel me. Girls have been expelled for less."

"Hell, I can't see anything wrong with that." Kling thought it over for a moment and then nodded emphatically. "There is nothing at all wrong with going on vacation with your fiancé—not boyfriend, if you please, but *fiancé*—especially if you plan on getting married soon."

"You make it sound worse than I did."

"Then your mind is as evil as your dean's."

"And yours, of course, is simon-pure."

Kling grinned. "Absolutely," he said.

"It still wouldn't work."

"Then give me another drink, and we'll resort to all kinds of subterfuge."

Claire poured two more hookers. "Here's to all kinds of subterfuge," she toasted. Together, they tossed off the shots, and she refilled the glasses.

"We could, of course, say you were having a baby."

"We could?"

"Yes. And that you were going to be confined to the hospital during finals, so could you please take them a little earlier? How does that sound?"

"Very good," Claire said. "The dean would appreciate that." She tossed off her drink and poured another.

"Go easy there," Kling advised. He drank his whiskey and held out his glass for a refill. "We need a clear head here—heads, I mean."

"Suppose..." Claire said thoughtfully.

"Um?"

"No, that wouldn't work."

"Let me hear it."

"No, no, it wouldn't work."

"What?"

"Well, I was thinking we could get married and say I had to miss finals because I was going on my honeymoon. How's that?"

"If you're trying to scare me," Kling said, "you're not."

"I thought you wanted to wait until I graduated."

"I do. Don't tempt me."

"Okay," Claire said. "Whoosh, I'm beginning to feel that booze."

"Keep a tight grip," Kling said. He thought silently for a moment. "Get me a pen and some paper, will you?"

"What for?"

"Letter to the dean," Kling said.

"All right," Claire answered.

She walked across the room to the secretary, and Kling said, "You wiggle very nice."

"Keep your mind on your work," Claire said.

"You *are* my work. You're my life's work."

Claire giggled and came back to him. She put her hands on his shoulders, leaned over, and kissed him fiercely on the mouth.

"You'd better go get the pen and paper," he said.

"I'd better," she answered. She walked away again, and again, he watched her. This time, she returned with a fountain pen and two sheets of stationery. Kling put the paper on the coffee table, uncapped the pen, and asked, "What's the dean's name?"

"Which one? We have several."

"The one in charge of vacations."

"None such."

"Permissions?"

"Anna Kale."

"Miss or Mrs.?"

"Miss," Claire said. "There are no such things as married deans."

"Dear Miss Kale," Kling said out loud as he wrote. "How's that for a beginning?"

"Brilliant," Claire said.

"Dear Miss Kale: I am writing to you on behalf of my daughter, Claire Townsend—"

"What's the penalty for forgery?" Claire asked.

"Shhhh," Kling said. "On behalf of my daughter, Claire Townsend, who requests permission to take her final examinations during the week of June third rather than during the scheduled examination period."

"You should have been a writer," Claire said. "You have a natural style."

"As you know," Kling went on, writing, "Claire is an honor student..." He paused. "Are you?"

"Phi Bete in my junior year," Claire said.

"A bloody genius," Kling said and then went back to the letter. "Claire is an honor student and can be trusted to take her exams without revealing their content to any students who will be tested at a later date. I would not make such an urgent request were it not for the fact that my sister is leaving for a tour of the West on June tenth—"

"A tour of the West!" Claire said.

"...a tour of the West on June tenth," Kling went on, "and has offered to take her niece with her. This is an opportunity that should not be bypassed, adding—I feel—more to a young girl's education than a strict compliance to schedule could offer. I hope you will agree the experience should be a rewarding one, and I know you would not put red tape into the way of a trip that would undoubtedly enrich one of your students. Trusting your decision will be the right one. I remain respectfully yours, Ralph

Townsend." Kling held the letter at arm's length. "How's that?" he asked.

"It'll make a fine Exhibit A for the state," Claire said.

"Screw the state," Kling said. "How about the letter?"

"My father hasn't got any sisters," Claire said.

"A slight oversight," Kling said. "What about the drama of the appeal?"

"Excellent," Claire said.

"Think she'll buy it?"

"What have we got to lose?"

"Nothing. I need an envelope." Claire rose and went to the secretary.

"Stop wiggling," he called after her.

"It's natural," she answered.

"It's *too* natural," Kling said. "That's the trouble."

He began doodling while she searched for an envelope. She found the envelope and started back across the room, walking as rigidly as she could, inhibiting the instinctive sway of her hips.

"That's better," Kling said.

"I feel like a robot."

She handed him the envelope, and he quickly scrawled *Miss Anna Kale* across its face. He folded the letter, put it into the envelope, sealed the envelope, and then handed it to Claire. "You are to deliver this tomorrow," he said. "Without fail. The fate of a nation hinges on your mission."

"I'm more interested in your doodling," Claire said, looking down at the drawing Kling had inked onto one of the stationery sheets.

"Oh, that," Kling said. He expanded his chest. "I was an ace in art appreciation, you know."

He had drawn a heart on the sheet of paper. He had put lettering into the heart. The completed masterpiece looked like this:

"For that," Claire said, "you deserve a kiss." She kissed him. She probably would have kissed him anyway, heart or no. Kling was, nonetheless, surprised and delighted. He accepted Claire's kiss, and her lips completely wiped out of his mind any connection he may have made between his own artistic endeavor and the tattoos found on the 87th's floaters.

He never knew how close he'd come to solving at least one mystery.

The second floater's name was Nancy Mortimer.

Her body had been identified by her parents who'd come from Ohio at the request of the police. She was thirty-three years old, a plain girl with simple tastes. She had left home two months ago, heading for the city. She had taken $2,000 in cash with her. She had told her parents she was going to meet a friend. If things went well, she'd told them, she would bring the friend home for them to meet.

Things, apparently, had not gone well.

The girl had been in the River Harb, according to the autopsy report, for at least a month.

And, according to the same report, the girl had died of arsenic poisoning.

There is an old Arab saying.

Actually, it is said by young Arabs, too. It fits many occasions, and so it is probably used with regularity. It is:

Show them the death, and they will accept the fever.

We don't have to look for hidden meanings in this gem of Arabian wisdom. The Freudian con men would probably impart thanatopsic values to what is undoubtedly an old folk saying. We don't have to do that. We can simply look at it for what it is and understand it for what it says.

It says:

Feed a man gravel, and he will then appreciate hardtack.

It says:

Bed a man down with an aged old crone, and he will then appreciate a middle-aged mah-jongg player.

It says:

Show them the death, and they will accept the fever.

Priscilla Ames had seen the death and was ready to accept the fever. In her native town of Phoenix, Priscilla Ames had gone out with many men who had considerably lowered her estimation of the species. She had seen the death, and after a considerably lengthy correspondence with a man whose address she'd got from a pen pal magazine, she was now ready to accept the fever.

To her delighted surprise, the fever turned out to be a delirium.

A blind date, after all, is something about which you exercise a little caution. When you travel away the hell from Phoenix to meet a man—even though you've already seen that man's picture, even though the picture looked good, but hadn't she sent a somewhat exotic pose, too, hadn't she cheated a little in the exchange of photos—you don't expect to meet a knight in shining armor. You approach cautiously.

Especially if you were Priscilla Ames, who had long ago dismissed such knights as figments of the imagination.

But here, by God, was a knight in shining armor.

Here, by all that was holy, was a shining resplendent man among men, a towering blond giant with a wide, white grin and laughing eyes, and a gentle voice, and a body like Apollo!

Here, by the saints, was the answer to every young maiden's prayer, the devoutly sought answer, the be-all and the end-all!

Here—was a man!

You could have knocked Priscilla over with a Mack truck. She had stepped off the plane, and there he was, coming toward her, grinning, and she had felt her heart quickening and then immediately thought, *No, he's made a mistake; it's the wrong man*, and then she knew it was the right man, the man she'd possibly been waiting for all her life.

That first day had sung, absolutely sung. Being in this magical, wonderful city, and drinking in the sights, and hearing the noise and the clamor, and feeling wonderfully alive again, and feeling above all his presence beside her, the tentative touch of his fingers on her arm, gentle with the promise of force. He had taken her to lunch and then to her hotel, and she had not been out of his sight since. It had been two weeks now, and she still could not adjust to the miracle of him. Ecstatically, she wondered if her life with this man would always be like this, would always be accompanied by a reckless headiness. Good Lord, she was drunk on him!

She stood before the mirror in her hotel bedroom now, waiting for him. She looked prettier, she felt. Her hair looked browner, and her eyes had more sparkle, and her breasts seemed fuller, and her hips seemed more feminine, and all because of him, all because of what he did to her. She wore his love like bright-white armor.

When she heard his knock on the door, she ran to open it. He was wearing a deep-blue trench coat, and the rain had loosened a wisp of his blond hair so that it hung boyishly on his forehead. She went into his arms instantly, her mouth reaching for his.

"Darling, darling," she said, and he held her close to him, and she could smell tobacco on him and aftershave, and she could smell, too, the close smell of rain-impregnated cloth.

"Pris," he said, and the word was a caress. No one had ever said her name the way he said it. No one had ever made it an important name, a name that was hers alone. He held her at arm's length and looked down at her. "You're beautiful," he said. "How come I'm so lucky?"

She never knew what to say in answer to his compliments. At first, she suspected he was simply flattering her. But there was sincerity and honesty about this man, and she could read truth in his eyes. Whatever her shortcomings, she felt this man honestly believed she was beautiful, and witty, and vivacious.

"I'll get an umbrella," she said.

"We don't need one," he answered. "It's a nice rain, Pris, warm. Do you mind? I like to walk in the rain. I'd like to walk in the rain with you."

"Whatever you say," she answered. She looked up at him. *I must look like a complete idiot*, she thought. *He must surely see adoration in my eyes. He must think I'm a stupid child instead of a grown woman.* "Where…where are we going tonight?" she asked.

"A wonderful place for dinner," he said. "We have a lot of talking to do."

"Talking?"

"Yes," he said. He saw the frown on her face, and his eyes twinkled. His fingers touched her forehead, smoothing out the frown. "Stop looking so serious," he chided. "Don't you know I love you?"

"Do you?" she asked, and there was fear in her eyes for a moment.

Then he pulled her to him and said, "Of course, I love you, Pris. Pris, I love you," and the fear vanished.

She buried her head in his shoulder, and there was a small smile of contentment on her mouth.

They walked in the rain.

It was, as he had promised, a warm rain. It touched the city gently. It roved the concrete canyons like a wistful maiden looking for her lost lover. It spoke in whispers, spoke to the buildings and the gutters and the park benches deserted and alone, and it spoke to the new green of the trees and to the growing things pushing to the sky, pushing through the warm, moist earth. It spoke in syllables as old as time, and it spoke to Priscilla and her man, spoke to two lovers who threaded their way across the city arm in arm, cradled in the warmth of the song of the rain.

He shook out his trench coat when they entered the restaurant. There was a pretty redheaded hatcheck girl, and he handed her his coat, and she smiled up at him, somewhat dazed by his good looks. But he turned from her without returning her smile, and he helped Priscilla out of her coat and then slung it over his arm and looked for the headwaiter.

The waiter led the couple to a table in the corner of the restaurant. The floors were decorated with a huge checkerboard tile in black and white. The walls were done in rich Italian mosaic, and clerestory windows threw the mottled light of dusk into the room. A candle burned brightly in the center of the round marble table. From somewhere near the bar, Pris heard the screech of a parrot. She craned her neck, looking past the tiers of huge apothecary jars filled with colored liquids—purples and reds and oranges and yellows and bright, vivid, living greens.

"Would you like to order now, sir?" the headwaiter asked.

"Some drinks first," he replied. "Rémy Martin for me," he said. "Pris?"

She was lost in the way he pronounced the drink, giving it the proper French twist. "What?" she asked.

"Something to drink?" he said, smiling.

"A whiskey sour," she said.

"Yes, miss," the headwaiter said. "A whiskey sour for the lady, and *what* was it for the gentleman, please?"

He looked up at the headwaiter, and for a moment, there was unmasked impatience in his eyes. And then, with something akin to cruelty, he viciously said, "Reeeeeemy Martin," pronouncing the words like a guttersnipe.

"Yes, sir. Of course, sir," the headwaiter said, and he bowed away from the table.

Priscilla watched her man, fascinated by his boldness and his quickness and his sureness.

"What was it you wanted to discuss?" she asked.

"First, the drinks," he said smiling. "Do you like this place?"

"Yes, it's wonderful. It's so different. There aren't any places like this in Phoenix."

"This is the most marvelous city in the world," he told her. "It's the only city that's really alive. And if you're in love, there's no place that can come near it. Even Paris. Paris is touted as the spot for lovers, but nothing can beat this city."

"Have you been to Paris?"

"I was there during the war," he said. "I was a commando."

"Wasn't that terribly dangerous?" she asked, feeling a foolish dread and knowing that the dread was idiotic because the danger was long past.

He shrugged. "Here are the drinks," he said.

The headwaiter brought their drinks and carefully placed them down. "Would you care to see a menu now?" he asked.

"Please."

He left the menus and tiptoed away.

Priscilla lifted her glass. He lifted his.

"To us," he said.

"Is that all?"

"That's everything, Pris," he said, and again, the sincerity shone in his eyes. "Everything I want. Us." He drank. "Good."

She drank with him, staring at him idiotically. "What…what did you want to discuss?"

"The date," he said simply.

"The…the date?"

"I want to marry you," he said, reaching across the table suddenly and clasping her hand under his. "Pris, you saw my plea; you answered my plea. Oh, Pris, there were dozens who answered it. Believe me, you have no idea how many lonely wom…lonely people there are in this world. But out of those dozens, and out of all the hundreds and thousands and millions of people who crawl over the face of this earth, *we* happened to come together. Like a couple of stars colliding in space, Pris, going their separate ways and then *wham*!" He lifted his hand from the table suddenly and slammed his fist into the open palm.

The sudden noise frightened her, but it also thrilled her. He was dynamic and unpredictable, and as one of the television brothers would have said, he certainly did have a flair for the dramatic.

"Like that," he said, "and there's a sudden shower of sparks. And, all at once, you've been part of my life always; all at once, I can't bear to be apart from you; all at once, I want you to be mine forever. I've got a job, you know that. A good job. I'm not the handsomest man in the world, but—"

"Oh, please," she said, "please—"

"…but I'm a hard worker, and I'll care for you always, Pris. This is why you came here to my city, to find me. And we've found each other, Pris, and I don't want to wait any longer. Not another minute."

"Wh…what do you mean?" she asked.

"I want to hear you say you'll marry me."

"You know I will," she answered, reaching across the table for his hand.

"Tomorrow," he said.

"Wh—"

"Tomorrow."

She looked at him steadily across the table. His eyes were glowing. His mouth looked sweet and tender.

"All right," she said in a small voice.

"Good." He grinned. "Dammit," he said, "I feel like kissing you." He rose suddenly, walked around the table, and kissed her just as the waiter approached to take their order.

The waiter didn't clear his throat. He simply stood there looking at them, watching them kiss. When they were finished, he said, "Did you…ah…care for anything else?"

They laughed and then gave the waiter their orders.

"I feel wonderful," she said.

"I feel great," he told her. "I feel as if I can lick this city with my bare hands. Pris, with you by my side, I can do anything, do you know that? Anything!"

"I…I'm glad you feel that way."

"Do you know why? Because I've got your love, and your love makes me feel strong."

"I…I feel strong, too," she said.

"How much do you love me?" he asked.

"Don't you know how much I love you?"

"How much?" he persisted.

"You're…you're the only thing that matters," she said.

"Pris," he said, his eyes gleaming now, "I've got something like ten thousand dollars in the bank. I'm going to ask for a vacation, by God! I'll ask for a month, and we'll go to Bermuda or someplace, how about that? Maybe Europe. What do you say, Pris?"

"I couldn't let you do that," she answered.

"Why not?"

"I couldn't let you spend your money so foolishly."

"My money?" he asked. A puzzled frown crossed his face. "*My* money? Pris, darling, once we're married, everything I've got is yours. Everything."

"Well, still—"

"Don't you look at it that way? Don't you feel we own everything together?"

"Certainly. But—"

"Then not another word about it. It's settled. We're going to Bermuda."

"I'd rather…I'd much rather start looking for a place…and…and furnishing it. We could take a short honeymoon, darling, but shouldn't we—"

"Of course, what an idiot I am! Of course, we've got to find a place of our own. My apartment is much too small, especially if we plan on a family later on." He looked at her as if he'd made a faux pas. "I…I remember your letter…the first one. You don't like children."

"Oh, I'd love your children," she said.

He smiled tremulously. "Well, I…I just wasn't sure. I…" He cocked his head to one side, as if his emotions were too much for him to bear, as if the pressure of his emotions had forced the movement of his head, the way a tidal wave causes a buoy to bob. "In any case, we've still got my ten thousand. That should furnish an apartment, all right."

"And my money," she added quietly.

"Your what?"

"The money I brought with me," she said.

"Oh, yes. I'd forgotten completely about it." He smiled indulgently. "What is it, darling, something like five hundred dollars?"

Her eyes opened wide in surprise. "You know very well it's closer to five *thousand* dollars," she said.

"You're joking!"

"I'm not. I'm serious." She grinned, enjoying his boyish surprise, feeling as if she had given him an unexpected present.

"You took...You carried so much *cash* with you?"

"Of course not. Don't you remember, darling? In one of my letters, I told you I would be closing out my bank account, and you suggested I carry it in traveler's checks."

"Yes, but I had no idea...five thousand dollars."

"It's really about forty-seven hundred," she said.

"Still...Honey, you've got to put that in the bank right away."

"Why?"

"So that it can start collecting interest. For God's sake, why do you need forty-seven hundred dollars in traveler's checks?"

"You're right," she said.

"Tomorrow, early in the morning," he said, "before the wedding, we'll open an account for you at my bank."

"A separate account, do you mean?" she asked.

"Naturally. It's your money, isn't it?"

"A little while ago, you said...you said when we were married everything you had was mine."

"Of course it is. You know that, darling. I meant every word I said."

"Then aren't you being a bit unfair?" she asked.

"Unfair? How?" He seemed very troubled. "What have I done, Pris? Have I said something wrong?"

"You said separate account."

"I don't understand."

She leaned across the table, and her eyes held his in a steady gaze. "Tomorrow," she said, "we'll be married. I'll go wherever you want to go and do whatever you want to do. I'll be yours—forever.

And that means completely. No games, no kidding. Forever. I've waited a long time for you, darling, and I expect this to be for keeps. Tomorrow morning, we'll go to your bank. I'll endorse the traveler's checks and deposit the forty-seven hundred dollars in your account."

He was already shaking his head.

"Yes," she said. "Yes."

"I can't allow you to do that," he told her. "I'm sorry, Pris. I want you, *not* a dowry."

"But it isn't a dowry," she said. "It's simply a stake in our future together. Don't you think I have a right to invest in our future?"

"Well—"

"You mustn't be stubborn about this, darling, really. It's the least I can bring to you. Besides, I'll feel as if all those lonely years of working and saving haven't gone for nothing. They'll have been worthwhile; they'll have been building for you…and for me."

"Well talk about it in the morning," he said.

"It's settled, as far as I'm concerned. That's the first thing we'll do, before we do anything else."

He seemed very worried about something.

She squeezed his hand and said, "What is it, darling?"

"I feel like a positive…I don't know…a…a moneylender or something!" he said vehemently.

"How silly you are," she said gently.

"To go into a bank with you and stand by while you endorse those checks and then deposit them in my account." He shook his head. "I'd feel like a…like a gigolo! No, I won't do it, Pris."

"Would it embarrass you?"

"Yes."

"I'll cash them at the hotel, then."

"I don't want you to cash them at all," he said. "But I suppose I'd feel a lot easier if you cashed them there."

"All right, I'll have them cashed at the hotel. I'll have the money in good American currency when you come to call for me. To take me to my wedding."

He grinned. "I suppose I am being foolish. All right, cash them at the hotel. Then we'll go to the bank, deposit the money, and away we go. To our wedding."

"There's a waiting period in this state, isn't there?" she asked.

"Yes. We'll drive out of the state. Look, let's do it right. I'll call for you at about ten. You'll have the checks cashed by then?"

"Yes."

"Good. We'll go to the bank and deposit them in my account, if that's what you want, and then we'll make a day of it. We'll have lunch downtown someplace—I know some very nice places—and then we'll drive out of the state. We'll just take our honeymoon as it comes, shall we? We'll stop wherever we feel like stopping."

"It sounds wonderful," she said.

"Good. Let's have another drink to it, shall we?"

He snapped his fingers for the waiter, and while they waited for him to come to their table, she leaned over and whispered the three most expensive words in the English language.

"I love you."

And he looked at her with tender guile and answered with the three cheapest words in the English language.

"I love you."

There was, in Teddy Carella, the constant fear that she didn't do enough for her husband.

Perhaps it was because she lacked the power of speech. She could not whisper the expensive words or the cheap words or any words. She could only show him how much she loved him, could only invent for him a thousand and one ways to show that she was his. She felt, you see, that she would eventually bore him. She felt that he would eventually seek a woman who could tell him the things his ears undoubtedly longed to hear—and she couldn't have been more wrong. Her face told him all he had to know.

Her devotion to invention, however, made her an excellent wife, a wife full of surprises, a wife who constantly delighted Carella and diverted Carella and made his life a day-by-day birthday party. In all truth, Teddy Carella would have been that kind of a wife even if she *could* speak. She was simply that kind of a person. Her ancestry was part Irish and part Scotch, but there was something of the Oriental philosophy in her attitude toward her husband. She wanted to please him. If he were pleased, she in turn would be pleased. She didn't have to read a book to know that love was a many-splendored thing.

And since her attitude was definitely Oriental, it was not surprising that her mind often returned to the jovial Charlie Chen and to the cherished butterfly design that adorned the wall of his shop.

What would Steve's reactions be if he came to her one night, found her in a flimsy nightgown, and upon lowering one of the delicate straps to kiss her shoulder, discovered there a lacy, black butterfly?

The prospect delighted her imagination.

The more she thought of it, the better the idea seemed. She was sure that Steve would be pleased. And, too, she was sure that Charlie Chen would be pleased. And, without a doubt, she herself would be pleased. There was something terribly risky and ridiculous about having a butterfly tattoo put on your shoulder. The idea was exciting. Even thinking about it, she could hardly contain her excitement.

But would it be very painful? she wondered.

Yes, it probably would be very painful. Although, Chen seemed like a man you could trust. Chen seemed like a man who would not hurt her. And Chen knew how much she loved her husband. That was important somehow. The butterfly would be a gift to Steve, and it should rightfully be tattooed by a man who knew and understood a woman's love for her man.

Pain be damned, she thought, *I shall do it!*

NOW!

She glanced at the clock. No, not now. Steve would be home for dinner soon, so not now. She went to the desk calendar and flipped the pages. She had a dental appointment day after tomorrow, but she was free all day tomorrow.

Would it really look attractive in a strapless gown?

Yes, if Chen did it delicately, a small black butterfly poised for flight.

She made her mental assignation. Tomorrow, after lunch, she would visit Charlie Chen.

And then, a live, dark butterfly poised for flight, she busied herself around the apartment, waiting for Steve, her secret humming inside her.

The young man had problems of his own.

He walked the streets of the city, and he concentrated on his problems, and he considered what happened to him, the greatest kind of good fortune.

The young man was dressed neatly and conservatively. He looked as if he might have money in the bank. He didn't look overly bright. He walked the streets of the city, and now that the rain had stopped, it wasn't so bad at all. People were beginning to appear in the streets, like victims of a siege after the shelling has stopped. The sky was still gray, but the clouds were tearing away in spots like gauzy cheesecloth, and the sun was trying desperately to push its way through. In the gutters, the accumulation of water sped for the sewers, carrying the miscellaneous refuse of the day. The kids rolled up their trouser legs and splashed in the water, stomping their feet. Store owners came out onto the sidewalk, stood looking up at the sky with hands on hips for a moment, and then went to roll up their awnings. A pair of lovers emerged from a dark hallway where they had stopped to wait out the rain. The girl's mouth had been kissed hard, and the boy's mouth carried lipstick, which had been bruised into the skin. Together, they walked briskly up the street, navigating the large puddles that dotted the sidewalk.

Everything stops, the young man thought. *The rain stops, and the sun comes out, and then the sun stops, and the rain begins. When will my particular problem stop?*

A boy on a bicycle rode past, his wheels creating hissing canopies of water as he raced alongside the sidewalk.

The young man watched the boy on the bicycle. He sighed heavily. There were two men standing on the sidewalk near the corner. One of the men was a redhead. The other man was tall, with dark hair, and he wore a dark-blue suit.

The young man gave them a cursory glance. As he approached them, the man in the blue suit stepped into his path.

"Excuse me," he said.

The young man looked up.

"My name is Charlie Parsons. I wonder if you'd do me a favor."

"What's that?" the young man asked.

"This fellow here," Parsons said, indicating the redhead, "has a gold coin, and I might be interested in buying it from him. Trouble is, I left my glasses home, and I can't read the date on it. I wonder if you'd be so kind."

The young man shrugged. "Well, I'm in sort of a hurry," he said.

"It'll only take a minute, and I'd certainly appreciate it."

"Well," the young man said, "where's the coin?"

The redhead produced a large gold coin. "Picked it up in Japan," he said. "I just got back from there. I was in the Army until last week. Just got discharged." The redhead grinned disarmingly. He seemed like a simple country boy. "My name's Frank O'Neill."

The young man simply nodded and took the coin. "What am I supposed to look for?" he asked.

"The date," Parsons told him. "Should be on the bottom there someplace."

"On the bott…Oh yes, here it is. 1801."

"1801?" Parsons said. "Are you sure?"

"That's what it says. 1801."

"Why, that's…" Parsons stopped himself.

O'Neill was looking at him. "That makes it pretty old, don't it?" he asked innocently.

Parsons cleared his throat. Obviously, he had stumbled upon something of real value and was now trying to hide his find. "No, that's not very old at all. In fact, I'd say that's a pretty common coin. The only surprising thing about it is that you were able to find a Russian coin in Japan."

The young man looked at Parsons and then at O'Neill. "Russia once had a war with Japan, you know," he said.

"Say, that's right," O'Neill said. "Bet that's how the coin happened to be there. Damn, if you can't pick up all kinds of junk in the interior of that country."

"I might still be interested in buying the coin," Parsons said guardedly. "Just as a curiosity piece, you understand. You know, a Russian coin that found its way to Japan."

"Well," O'Neill said, "I got it for a pack of cigarettes." His candid naïveté was remarkable. "That's all it cost me."

"I couldn't let you have more than ten dollars for it," Parsons said judiciously. In an aside, he winked at the young man.

The young man stared at him, a puzzled expression on his face.

"I'd say you just bought yourself a gold coin," O'Neill said, grinning.

Parsons reached into his wallet, trying to hide his haste. He pulled out a twenty-dollar bill and handed it to O'Neill. "Do you have any change?" he asked.

"No, I don't," O'Neill said. "Let me have the bill, and I'll cash it in that cigar store."

Parsons gave him the bill, and O'Neill went into the cigar store on the corner. As soon as he was gone, Parsons turned to the young man.

"Jesus," he said, "do you know what that coin is worth?"

"No," the young man said.

"At least two hundred dollars! And he's letting me have it for ten!"

"You're pretty lucky," the young man said.

"Lucky, hell. I spotted him for a hick from the minute I saw him. I'm just wondering what else he's got to sell."

"I doubt if he's got anything else," the young man said.

"I don't. He's just back from Japan. Who knows what else he may have picked up? I'm going to pump him when he gets back."

"Well, I'll be running along," the young man said.

"No, stick around, will you? I may need your eyesight. What a time to forget my glasses, huh?"

O'Neill was coming out of the cigar store. He had got two tens for the twenty, and he handed one of the tens and the gold coin to Parsons. The other ten he put into his pocket. "Well," he said, "much obliged." He started to go, and Parsons laid a hand on his arm.

"You said…uh…that you could get all kinds of junk in the interior. What…uh…did you have in mind?"

"Oh, all kinds of junk," O'Neill said.

"Like what?"

"Well, I picked up some pearls," O'Neill said. "As a matter of fact, I'm sorry I did."

"Why?"

"Damn things cost me a fortune, and I could use some money right now."

"How much did they cost you?" Parsons asked.

"Five hundred dollars," O'Neill said, as if that were all the money in the world.

"Real pearls?"

"Sure. Black ones."

"Black pearls?" Parsons asked.

"Yeah. Here, you want to see them?" He reached into his pocket and pulled out a leather bag. He unloosened the drawstrings on the bag and poured some of its contents into the palm of his hand. The pearls were not exactly black. They glowed with gray luminescence.

"There they are," O'Neill said.

"That bag is full of them?" Parsons asked, taking one of the pearls and studying it.

"Yeah. Got about a hundred of them in there. Fellow I bought them from was an old Jap."

"Are you sure they're genuine?"

"Oh, sure," O'Neill said.

"They're not paste?"

"Would I pay five hundred dollars for paste?"

"Well, no. No, I guess not." Parsons looked hastily to the young man. Then he turned to O'Neill. "Are you…are you…Did you want to sell these?"

"I tell you," O'Neill said, "the Army discharged me here, and I live down South. I lost all my money on the boat took us back, and I'll be damned if I know how I'm going to get home."

"I'd be…ah…happy to give you five hundred dollars for these," Parsons said. Quickly, he licked his lips, as if his mouth had suddenly gone dry. "Provided they're genuine."

"Oh, they're real, all right. But I couldn't let you have them for five hundred."

"That's what they cost you," Parsons pointed out.

"Sure, but I had the trouble of making the deal and of carting them all the way back to the States. I wouldn't let them go for less than a thousand."

"Well, that's kind of high," Parsons said. "We don't even know they're genuine. They may be paste."

"Hell, I wouldn't try to stick you," O'Neill said.

"I've been stuck before," Parsons said. "After all, I don't know you from a hole in the wall."

"That's true," O'Neill said, "but I hope you don't think I'd let you buy these pearls without having a jeweler look at them first."

Parsons looked at him suspiciously. "How do I know the jeweler isn't a friend of yours?"

"You can pick any jeweler you like. I won't even come into the shop with you. I'll give you the pearls, and I'll wait outside. Listen, these are the real articles. Only reason I'm letting you have them so cheap is because I don't want to fool around. I want to go home."

"What do you think?" Parsons asked, turning to the young man.

"I don't know," the young man said.

"Will you come with us to a jeweler?"

"What for?"

"Come along," Parsons said. "Please."

The young man shrugged. "Well, all right," he said.

They walked up the street until they came to a jewelry shop. The sign outside said: REPAIRS, APPRAISALS.

"This should do it," Parsons said. "Let me have the pearls."

O'Neill handed him the sack.

"You coming?" Parsons asked the young man.

"All right," the young man said.

"You'll see," O'Neill said. "He'll tell you they're worth a thousand dollars."

Together, Parsons and the young man went into the shop. O'Neill waited outside on the sidewalk.

The jeweler was a wizened old man bent over a watch. He did not look up. He kept his brow squeezed tight against the black eyepiece, and he picked at the watch like a man pulling meat from a lobster claw. Parsons cleared his throat. The jeweler did not look up. Together, they waited. A cuckoo clock on the wall chirped the time. It was 2:00 P.M.

Finally, the jeweler looked up. He opened his eyes wide, and the eyepiece fell into his open palm.

"Yes?" he asked.

"I'd like some pearls appraised," Parsons said.

"Where are they?"

"Right here," Parsons said, extending the sack.

The jeweler loosened the drawstrings. He shook a few of the smoky gray globes into the palm of his hand.

"Nice size," he said. "Nice sheen. Nice smoothness. What do you want to know?"

"Are they real?"

"They're not paste, I can tell you that immediately." He nodded. "Impossible to say whether they're cultured or genuine Oriental without having them x-rayed, though. I'd have to send them out of the shop for that."

"How much are they worth?" Parsons asked.

The jeweler shrugged. "If they're cultured, you can get between ten and twenty-five dollars for each pearl. If they're genuine Oriental, the price is much higher."

"How much higher?"

"Judging from the size of these, I'd say between a hundred and two hundred for each pearl. At least a hundred." He paused. "How much did you want for them?"

"A thousand," Parsons said.

"You've got a sale," the jeweler answered.

"I'm not selling," Parsons said. "I'm buying."

"How many are in that sack?" the jeweler asked. "About seventy-five pearls?"

"A hundred," Parsons said.

"Then you can't go wrong. Even if they're cultured, you'd get at least ten dollars for each pearl—so there's your thousand right there. And if they're genuine Oriental, you stand to make a phenomenal profit. If they're genuine Oriental, you can get back ten times your investment. I'd have them x-rayed at once, if I were you."

Parsons grinned. "Thank you," he said. "Thanks a lot."

"Don't mention it," the jeweler said. He put his eyepiece back in place and bent over his watch again.

Parsons took the young man to one side. "What do you think?" he asked.

"Looks like a good deal," the young man said.

"I know. Listen, I can't let this hick get away from me."

"He's willing to sell. What makes you think he'll try to get away?"

"That's just it. If these pearls are genuine Oriental, he's sitting on a fortune. I've got to buy them before he has them x-rayed himself."

"I see what you mean," the young man said.

"The trouble is, I live in the next state. By the time I got to my bank, it'd be closed. This fellow isn't going to wait until tomorrow, that's for sure."

"I guess not," the young man said.

"Do you live in the city?"

"Yes."

"Do you bank here?"

"Yes."

"Have you got a thousand dollars in the bank?"

"Yes."

"I hate to do this," Parsons said.

"Hate to do what?"

Parsons smiled. "I hate to cut you in on such a sweet deal."

"Would you?" the young man asked, interest showing in his eyes.

"What choice do I have? If I asked our hick to wait until tomorrow, I'd lose him."

"Fifty-fifty split?" the young man asked.

"Now, wait a minute," Parsons said.

"Why not? I'll be putting up the money."

"Only until tomorrow. Besides, he's my hick. You wouldn't have known anything about this if I hadn't stopped you."

"Sure, but you can't buy those pearls if I don't go to the bank."

"That's true." Parsons' eyes narrowed. "How do I know you won't take the pearls and then refuse to sell me my half tomorrow?"

"I wouldn't do a thing like that," the young man said.

"I want your address and telephone number," Parsons said.

"All right," the young man said. He gave them to Parsons, and Parsons wrote them down.

"How do I know these are legitimate?" Parsons asked. "Let me see your driver's license."

"I don't drive. You can check it in the phone book." He turned to the jeweler. "Have you got an Isola directory?"

"Never mind," Parsons said. "I trust you. But I'll be at your apartment first thing tomorrow morning to give you my five hundred dollars and to get my share of the pearls."

"All right," the young man said. "I'll be there."

"God, this is a great deal, isn't it? If they're genuine, we'll be rich. And if they're cultured, we break even. We can't lose."

"It's a good deal," the young man agreed.

"Let's get to the bank before he changes his mind."

O'Neill was waiting for them outside. "Well?" he asked.

"He said they're not paste," Parsons told him.

"See? What'd I tell you? Did he say they're worth a thousand?"

"He said they might be worth about that."

"Well, do we have a deal, or don't we?"

"I'll have to go home for my passbook," the young man said.

"All right. We'll go with you."

The three men hailed a cab, and the cab took them uptown. The young man got out, and the cab waited. When he came down again, he had his bankbook with him. He gave the cabbie instructions, and the three men drove to the bank. They all got out then, and Parsons paid the cabbie. The young man went into the bank, and when he came out, he had a thousand dollars in cash with him.

"Here's the money," he said.

Parsons grinned happily.

The young man handed the thousand dollars to O'Neill.

"And here're the pearls," O'Neill said, reaching into his pocket and handing the young man a leather sack. "I'm certainly much obliged to you fellows. This means I'll be able to go home."

"Not for a long while," the young man said.

O'Neill looked up. He was staring into the open end of a .38 Detective's Special. "What?" he said.

The young man grinned. "The old diamond switch," he said, "only with pearls. You've got my thousand, and the pearls in this sack you gave me are undoubtedly paste. Where are the real ones the jeweler appraised?"

"Listen," Parsons said, "you're making a mistake, Mac. You're—"

"Am I?" The young man was already frisking O'Neill. In two seconds, he located the sack of real pearls. "Tomorrow morning, I'd be sitting around in my apartment waiting for my *partner* to arrive with his five hundred dollars. Only, my partner would never show up. My partner would be out spending his share of the thousand dollars he conned from me."

"This is the first time we ever done anything like this," O'Neill said, beginning to panic.

"Is it? I've got a few other people who may be willing to identify you," the young man said. "Come on, we're taking a little ride."

"Where to?" Parsons asked.

"To the 87th Precinct," the young man said.

The young man's name was Arthur Brown.

The tattoo parlor was near the Navy yards, and so the specialties of the house were anchors, mermaids, and fish. There were also dagger designs, and ship designs, and mothers in hearts.

The man who ran the place was called "Popeye." He was called Popeye because a drunken sailor had once jabbed out his left eye with his own tattooing needle. Judging from Popeye's present condition, he may very well have been drunk himself when he'd lost his eye. He was certainly ossified now. Carella reflected upon the man's profession and concluded that he wouldn't trust him to remove a small splinter with a heated needle, no less decorate his flesh with a tattooing tool.

"Come and go, come and go," Popeye said. "All th' time. In an' out, in an' out. From all ov' the worl'. I decorate 'em. Me. I color their fleshes."

Carella was not interested in those who came and went from all over the world. He was interested in what Popeye had told him just a few minutes before.

"This couple," he said, "tell me more about them."

"Han'some guy," Popeye said. "Ver' han'some. Big, tall, blond feller. Walk like a king. Rish. You can tell when they rish. He had money, this feller."

"You tattooed the girl?"

"Nancy. Tha' was her name. Nancy."

"How do you know?"

"He called her that. I heard him."

"Tell me exactly what happened?"

"She in trouble? Nancy in trouble?"

"She's in the biggest kind of trouble," Carella said. "She's dead."

"Oh." Popeye squinched up his face and looked at Carella with his good eye. "Tha's a shame," he said. "Li'l Nancy's dead. Automobile accident?"

"No," Carella said. "Arsenic."

"Wha's that?" Popeye asked.

"A deadly poison."

"Too bad. Li'l girls should'n take poison. She cried, you know? When I was doin' the job. Bawled like a baby. Big han'some bassard jus' stood there an' grinned. Like as if I was brandin' her for him. Like as if I was puttin' a trademark or somethin' on her. Sick as a dog, poor li'l Nancy."

"What do you mean, sick?"

"Sick, sick."

"How?"

"Pukin'," Popeye said.

"The girl vomited?" Carella asked.

"Right here in th' shop," Popeye said. "Got th' can all slobbed up."

"When was this?"

"They'd jus' come from lunch," Popeye said. "She was talkin' about it when they come in th' shop. Said they didn't have no Chinese res'rants in her hometown."

"Is there a Chinese restaurant in the neighborhood?"

"One aroun' th' corner. Looks like a dump, but has real good food. Cantonese. You dig Cantonese?"

"What else did she say?"

"Said th' food was ver' spicy. Tha' figgers, don't it?"

"Go on."

"Han'some said he wanted a tattoo on the li'l girl's hand. A heart an' N-A-C."

"He said that?"

"Yeah."

"Why N-A-C?"

Popeye cocked his head so that his dead socket stared Carella directly in the face. "Why, tha's their names," he said.

"What do you mean, names?"

"'Nitials, I mean. *N* is her initial. *N* for Nancy."

Carella felt as if he'd been struck by lightning.

"The *A* is jus' 'and,' you know. Nancy *and* Chris. Tha' was his name. Chris. N. A. C."

"Goddammit!" Carella said. "Then the Proschek girl's tattoo meant *Mary* and Chris. I'll be a son of a bitch!"

"Wha'?" Popeye said.

"How do you know his name was Chris?" Carella asked.

"She said so. When he said, 'N-A-C,' she said, 'Why don't we put th' whole names, Nancy and Chris?' Tha's what she said."

"What did he say?"

"Said there wasn't enough space. Said it was just a tiny li'l heart. Hell, that li'l girl was goofy about him. He'da tole her to lay down an' take off her bloomers, she'da done it ri' here in the shop."

"You said she cried while you were working on her?"

"Yeah. Bawled like a baby. Hurt like hell."

"Were you drunk?"

"Me? Drunk? Hell, no. Wha' makes you think I was drunk?"

"Nothing. What happened next?"

"She was cryin', and I was working, and then all of a sudden, she fells sick. Han'some looked kind of worried. He kep' tryin' to rush her out of the shop, but the poor girl had to puke, you know? So I took her in back. Slobbed up the whole damn can."

"Then what?"

"He wanted to take her away. Kep' sayin', 'Come on, Nancy, we'll go to my place. Come on.' She wouldn' go withim. Said she wanted me to finish th' tattoo. Game kid, huh?"

"Did you finish it?"

"Yeah. She was sick as hell all the way through. You could see she was tryin' to keep from pukin' again." Popeye paused. "But I finished it. Nice job, too. Han'some paid me, an' away they went."

"Into a car?"

"Yeah."

"What make?"

"I dinn notice," Popeye said.

"Goddamn," Carella said.

"I'm sorry," Popeye said. "I dinn notice."

"Did she mention the man's last name? This Chris fellow."

Popeye thought for a moment. "Yeah, yeah," he said. "She did. She said something about the future Mrs. Somebody."

"Mrs. *Who*?" Carella asked.

"I don't remember."

"Goddamn," Carella said again. He snorted heavily. He bit his lower lip. "Can you give me a full description of the man?" he asked finally.

"Much's I can remember," Popeye said.

"Blond hair," Carella said, "right?"

"Yeah."

"Long or short?"

"Average."

"He wasn't wearing a crew cut or anything like that?"

"No."

"All right, what about his eyes? What color?"

"Blue, I think. Or gray. One or th' other."

"What kind of a nose?"

"Good nose. Not long, not short. Good nose. He was a han'some guy."

"Mouth?"

"Good mouth."

"Was he smoking?"

"No."

"Any scars or birthmarks on his face?"

"No."

"Anywhere on his body?"

"I dinn undress him," Popeye said.

"I meant visible. On his hands perhaps? Tattoos? Any tattoos on his hands?"

"Nope."

"What was he wearing?"

"Topcoat. This was back in February, you know. A black topcoat. Had a kind of a red lining. Red silk, I think, and those straps you slip your hands through."

"What straps?"

"Inside the coat. You know, so you can slip it over your shoulders while you're at the track. That's what I mean."

"What kind of a suit?"

"A tweed. Gray."

"Shirt?"

"White."

"Tie?"

"Black tie. I remember asking him if he was in mourning. He jus' grinned."

"He would, the bastard. Are you sure you can't remember the make of the car he was driving? That would be very helpful."

"I ain't good on cars," Popeye said.

"Did you happen to notice the license plate?"

"Nope."

"But I'll bet you can tell me what kind of a tie-clasp he was wearing," Carella said, sighing.

"Yeah. Silver bar with a horse's head on it. Nice. I figured him for a horseplayer."

"What else do you remember?"

"Tha's about it."

"Did they mention where they were going?"

"Yeah. To his place. He said she could lay down there an' he'd get her something cool to put on her forehead."

"Where? Did he say where?"

"No. He only said his place. That could be anyplace in the city."

"You're telling me?" Carella asked.

"I'm sorry," Popeye said. "Guy wants to take care of a girl with a stomach ache, that's his business. Wants to get her something for her head, ain't none of my affair."

"He got her something for her *feet*," Carella said.

"Huh?"

"A hundred pound weight to carry her to the bottom of the river."

"He drowned her?" Popeye asked. "You mean he drowned that nice li'l girl?"

"No, he—"

"Bravest li'l thing ever come in here. Even the sailors I get whimper. She bawled, an' she got sick, but she come right back for more. That takes guts. To come back for more when you're so scared you're sick."

"You don't know just how much guts it took," Carella said.

"An' he drowned her, huh? How do you like that?"

"I didn't say he—"

"What a way to die," Popeye said, shaking his head. His nose was red and bulging with aggravated veins. His one good eye was watery and bloodshot. His breath stank of cheap wine. "What a way to die," he repeated. "Drownin.'"

"You're well on the way," Carella said.

Then he thanked him and left the shop.

Chris Donaldson had already fed her the arsenic.

He had fed it to her in a half-dozen dishes—the tea, the fried rice, the chow mein, every dish he could get to while she was in the ladies' room. When the food had come, he'd simply said, "Let's wash up," and then he'd taken Priscilla by the elbow and led her away from the table. He'd doubled back almost instantly and done his work, and she had consumed the odorless and almost tasteless arsenic with apparent relish.

They had gone to the Chinese restaurant directly after they'd left the bank. They had deposited Priscilla's money in his account, and now she had consumed the arsenic, and now it was all a matter of time.

He watched her with the flat look of a reptile, a slight smile on his face. He hoped she would not get sick too soon, like the last one. That had been an embarrassing episode. Even beautiful women lost all their charm when they became violently ill, and the women he had murdered, and was now murdering, were far from beautiful.

"That was good," Priscilla said.

"More tea, darling?" he asked.

"Yes, please." He poured from the small, round pot. "Don't you like tea?" she asked. "You haven't had any."

"Not particularly," he said. "I'm a coffee drinker."

She took the cup from him. "Did you put sugar in it?" she asked.

"Yes," he said. "Everything's in it," and he smiled at his own grim humor.

"You'll make a good husband," Priscilla said. She felt full and warm and drowsy. That afternoon she would be married. She felt lazy and content and at complete peace with the world. "You'll make a wonderful husband."

"I'm going to try my damnedest," he said. "I'm going to make you the happiest woman in the world."

"I'm the happiest woman in the world right now."

"I want everyone to know you're mine," Donaldson said. "Everyone. I want to shout it at them. I want big signs telling them."

Priscilla grinned.

He watched her grin, and he thought, *Do you know you've been poisoned, my dear? Do you know what metallic poisoning is?* He watched her, and he felt neither pity nor compassion. It would not be long now. A few hours at the most. Tonight he would dispose of her, the way he had disposed of the others. There was just one thing remaining, one concession to his ego. Like a great painter, he must sign his work. He must lead her into helping him sign his work.

"I get crazy ideas sometimes," he said.

"Ah-ha," she answered. "Now he tells me there's insanity in his family. A few hours before the wedding and he trots out the skeletons."

"I really *do* get crazy ideas," he persisted, as if his speech were rehearsed, a speech that had worked for him before and that he was sure would work now, annoyed because she had interrupted the smooth, rehearsed flow of his speech with her silly witticism. "Like I...I want to brand you. I want to put my name on you so that people will know you're mine."

"They'll know, anyway. They can see it in my eyes."

"Yes, but...Well, it's silly, I admit it. It's crazy. Didn't I tell you it was crazy? Didn't I warn you?"

"If I were a cow, darling," she said, "I wouldn't at all mind being branded."

"There must be some way," he said, as if mulling the problem over. He reached across the table for her hand, toyed with her fingers. "Oh, I don't mean a red-hot branding iron. Pris, that would kill me. Any pain to you would kill me. But..." He stopped, studying her hand. "Say," he said. "Saaaay..."

"What?"

"A tattoo. How about that?"

Priscilla smiled. "A what?"

"A tattoo."

"Well..." Priscilla was puzzled. "What about a tattoo?"

"How would you like one?"

"I wouldn't," she said firmly.

"Oh." His voice fell.

"Why on earth would I want a tattoo?"

"No," he said. "Never mind."

She stared at him, confused. "What's the matter, darling?"

"Nothing."

"Are you angry?"

"No."

"You are, I can see it. Do you...do you *want* me to have a...a tattoo?"

"Yes," he said.

"I'm not sure I understand."

"A small one. Someplace on your hand." He took her hand again. "Right here perhaps, between the thumb and forefinger."

"I…I'm afraid of needles," Priscilla said.

"Then forget it." He stared at the tablecloth. "Finish your tea, won't you, darling?" he said, and he smiled up at her, a defeated, boyish smile.

"If I…" She stopped, thinking. "It's just that I'm afraid of needles."

"It doesn't hurt at all, you know," he said. "I thought perhaps a little heart. With our initials in it. Priscilla and Chris. P-A-C. So that everyone would know. Everyone would know you're my woman."

"I'm afraid of needles," she said.

"It doesn't hurt," he assured her.

"Chris, I…I'll do anything else you want. Anything, really. It's just that I've always been afraid of needles. Even getting a shot from the doctor."

"Then forget it," he said pleasantly.

She looked into his eyes. "You're angry, aren't you?"

"No, no, not at all."

"You are."

"Pris, really, I'm not. I'm just a little…disappointed."

"In me?"

"No, of course not in you. How could I be disappointed in you?"

"In what then?"

"Well, I thought you'd like the idea."

"I *do* like it, Chris. I *want* people to know I belong to you. But—"

"Yes, I know."

"I feel like such a baby."

"No, you're perfectly right. If you have a fear of—"

"Chris, please, I feel so silly. It probably..." She bit her lip. "It probably doesn't hurt at all."

"Not at all," he said.

"I am...I am being a baby."

"Forget it," he said, but there was an aloofness about him that chilled her. Desperately, she wanted to reach him again, wanted to be safe and secure in the warmth of his respect.

"I'll...I'll do whatever you say," she told him.

"No, don't be ridiculous," he said. He snapped his fingers and called, "Waiter," and to her, he said, "Let's get out of here."

"I'll do it, Chris. I'll...I'll do it. The tattoo. Whatever you want."

His eyes softened. He took her hands and said, "Would you, Pris? It would really make me very happy."

"I want to make you happy," she said.

"Good. There's a tattoo parlor right on the edge of Chinatown. It won't hurt, Pris. I can promise you that."

She nodded. "I'm petrified," she said.

"Don't be. I'll be right there with you."

She covered her mouth and swallowed hard. "This food was awfully heavy," she said. She smiled apologetically. "Very good, but heavy. I feel a little queasy."

He looked at her, and there was concern in his eyes. The waiter approached the table, quietly depositing the check face-down. Donaldson picked up the check, glanced at it, left a tip on the table, and then took Priscilla's arm. He paid the check at the cashier's booth.

As they left the restaurant, he said, "Do you know the story about the man who goes to a Chinese brothel?"

"Oh, Chris," she said.

"He goes there, and then the madam is surprised to see him returning five minutes later. She says to him, 'But you were here just five minutes ago with Ming Toy, our most beautiful girl.' And the fellow looks at her and says, 'Well, you know how it is with a Chinese meal.'"

Priscilla laughed and then sobered almost instantly. "I still feel queasy," she said.

He took her elbow and glanced at her quickly. Then he quickened his pace and said, "We'd better hurry."

To say that Charlie Chen was surprised to see Teddy Carella would be a complete understatement.

The door to his shop had been closed, and he heard the small tinkle of the bell when the door opened, and he glanced up momentarily and then lifted his hulk from the chair in which he sat smoking and went to the front of the shop.

"Oh!" he said, and then his round face broke into a delighted grin. "Pretty detective lady come back," he said. "Charlie Chen is much honored. Charlie Chen is much flattered. Come, sit down, Mrs. . . ." He paused. "Charlie Chen forget name."

Teddy touched her lips with the tips of her fingers and then shook her head. Chen stared at her, uncomprehending. She repeated the gesture.

"You can't talk, maybe?" he asked. "Laryngitis?"

Teddy smiled, shook her head, and then her hand traveled swiftly from her mouth to her ears, and Chen at last understood.

"Oh," he said. "Oh." His eyes clouded. "Very sorry, very sorry."

Teddy gave a slight shake of her head and a slight lift of her shoulders and a slight twist of her hands, explaining to Chen that there was nothing to be sorry for.

"But you understand me?" he asked. "You know what I say?"

Yes, she nodded.

"Good. You most beautiful lady ever come into Charlie Chen's poor shop. I speak this from my heart. Beauty is not plentiful in the world today. There is not much beauty. To see true beauty, this gladdens me. Makes me very happy, very happy. I talk too fast for you?"

Teddy shook her head.

"You read my lips?" He nodded appreciatively. "That very clever, very clever. Why you come visit Charlie Chen?"

Teddy looped her thumbs together and then moved her hands as if they were in flight.

"The butterfly?" Chen asked, astounded. "You want the butterfly?"

Yes, she nodded, delighted by his response.

"Oh," he said, "ohhhhhh," as if her acknowledgment were the fulfillment of his wildest dream. "I make very pretty. I make pretty big butterfly."

Teddy shook her head.

"No big butterfly? Small butterfly?"

Yes.

"Ah, very clever, very clever. Delicate butterfly for pretty lady. Big butterfly no good. Small, little, pretty butterfly better. You very smart. You very beautiful, and you very smart. I do. Come. Come in. Please. Come in."

He parted the curtains leading to the back of the shop and then gallantly bowed and stepped aside while Teddy passed through. She went directly to the butterfly design pinned to the wall. Chen smiled and then seemed to notice for the first time the calendar with its naked woman on the other wall.

"Excuse other pretty lady, please," he said. "Stupid sons do."

Teddy glanced at the calendar and smiled.

"You decide color?" Chen asked.

She nodded.

"Which?"

Teddy touched her hair.

"Black? Ah, good. Black very good. Little, black butterfly. Come. Sit. I do. No pain. Charlie Chen be very careful."

He sat her down, and she watched him, beginning to get a little frightened now. Deciding to get one's shoulder decorated was one thing. Going ahead with it was another thing again. She watched his movements as he walked around the shop preparing his tools. Her eyes were saucer wide.

"You frightened?" he asked.

She gave a very small nod.

"No be. Everything go hunky-dory. I promise. Very clean, very sanitary, very harmless." He smiled. "Very painless, too."

Teddy kept watching him, her heart in her mouth.

"I use very-deep black. Black no good unless really black. Otherwise is gray. Life is all full of grays, pretty lady. No sharp whites, no sharp blacks. All grays. Very sad, life is." Chen brought a pencil and a sheet of paper to the table. He drew several circles on it, one the size of a dime, the next the size of a nickel, then the size of a quarter, and lastly, the size of a half-dollar.

"Which size do you want butterfly?" he asked.

Teddy studied the circles.

"Biggest one too big, no?" Chen asked.

Teddy nodded.

"Okay. We disintegrate." He made a large cross over the half-dollar circle.

"Littlest one too little, yes?" he asked.

Again, Teddy nodded.

"Poof!" Chen said, and he crossed out the dime-sized circle. "Which of these two?" he asked, pointing to the nickel and the quarter.

Teddy shrugged.

"I think bigger one, no? Then Charlie can do nice lace on wings. Too small is difficult. Can do, but is difficult. Bigger one, we get nice effect, all lacy. Very pretty." He cocked his head to one side and extended his forefinger. "But not too big. Too big no good." He nodded. "Most things in life too big. Gray and too big. People forget blacks and whites. People forget little things. I tell you something."

Teddy watched him, wondering if he were talking to put her at ease, realizing at the same time that he was succeeding. The panic she had felt just a few moments earlier was rapidly dissolving.

"You want listen?" Chen asked.

Teddy nodded.

"I was married very pretty lady. Shanghai. You know Shanghai?"

Teddy nodded again.

"Very nice city, Shanghai. I was tattoo there, too. Very skill art in China, tattoo. I tattoo many people. Then I marry very pretty lady. Prettiest lady in all Shanghai. Prettiest lady in all China! She give me three sons. She make me very happy. Life blacks and whites with her. Sharp, good contrast. Everything clear and bright. Everything clean. No grays. Big concern for little things. Very joyous, very happy." Chen was nodding, lost in his reminiscence. His eyes had glazed somewhat, and Teddy watched him, feeling a sadness in the man even before he spoke his next words.

"She die," he said. "Life very funny. Good things die early; bad ones never die. She die. Life is grey again. Have three sons, but no laughter. No more lights in Shanghai. No more people talking. No more happiness. Only empty Charlie Chen. Empty."

He paused, and she wanted to reach out to touch his hand, to comfort him.

"I come here America. Very good country. I have trade, tattoo." He wagged his head. "I get by, make living. Send oldest son to college; he not so stupid, as I say. Younger ones good in school, too. I learn to live. Only one thing missing. Beauty. Very hard to find beauty." Chen smiled. "You bring beauty to my shop. I am very grateful. I do beautiful butterfly. My fingers wither and dry if I do not do beautiful butterfly. This I promise. I promise, too, no pain. This, too, I promise. You relax, yes? You unbutton blouse just a little, move off shoulder." He paused. "Which shoulder? Left or right? Very important to decide."

Teddy touched her left shoulder.

"Ah, no, butterfly on left shoulder bad omen. We do right, okay? You no mind? We put pretty, small, black, lacy butterfly on right shoulder, okay?"

Teddy nodded. She unbuttoned the top button of her blouse and then dipped the blouse off her shoulder.

Chen looked up from his needle suddenly.

The bell over his front door had just sounded.

Someone had entered the shop.

Chen may not have recognized the tall, blond man were it not for the fact that Teddy Carella was in the back of his shop, waiting to be tattooed.

For whereas the handsome blond had been an impressive figure, Chen had only seen him once, and that had been a long time ago. But now, with Teddy in the rear of the shop, with Chen keenly reminded of Teddy's relationship to a husband who was a cop, he recognized the blond man the instant he stepped through the beaded curtains to confront him.

"Yes?" he said, and he saw the man's face, and curiously, he automatically began thinking in Chinese. *This is the man the detective seeks*, he thought. *The husband of the beauty who now waits to be tattooed. This is the man.*

"Hello, there," Donaldson said. "We've got some work for you."

Chen's eyes fled to the girl beside Donaldson. She was not pretty. Her hair was a mousy brown, and her eyes were a faded brown, and she wore glasses, and she peered through the glasses, she was not pretty at all. She also looked a little sick. There was a tight, drawn expression to her face, and her skin was pallid. She did not look well at all.

"What kind of work, please?" Chen asked.

"A tattoo," Donaldson said, smiling.

Chen nodded. "A tattoo for the gentleman, yes, sir," he said.

"No," Donaldson corrected, "a tattoo for the lady," and there was no longer the slightest doubt in Chen's mind. This was the man. A girl was dead, perhaps because of this man. Chen eyed him narrowly. This man was dangerous.

"You will sit down, please?" he asked. "I be with you in one minute."

"Hurry, won't you?" Donaldson said. "We haven't got much time."

"I be with you two shakes," Chen said, and he parted the curtains and moved quickly to the back of the shop. He walked directly to Teddy. She saw the anxiety on his face immediately. She gave him her complete attention at once. Something had happened, and Chen was very troubled.

In a whisper, he said, "Man here. One your husband wants. Do you understand?"

For a moment, she didn't understand. *Man here? One my husband*...And then the meaning became clear, and she felt a sudden chill at the base of her spine, felt her scalp begin to prickle.

"He here with girl," Chen said. "Want tattoo. You understand?"

She swallowed hard, and then she nodded.

"What I should do?" Chen asked.

"I...I don't feel too well," Priscilla Ames said.

"This won't take but a moment," Donaldson assured her.

"Chris, I really don't feel well. My stomach..." She shook her head. "Do you suppose that food was all right?"

"I'm sure it was, darling. Look, we'll get the tattoo, and then we'll stop for a bromo or something, all right? We have a long drive ahead, and I wouldn't want you to be sick."

"Chris, do we…do we have to get the tattoo? I feel awful. I've never felt like this before in my life."

"It'll pass, darling. Perhaps the food was a little too rich."

"Yes, it must have been something. Chris, I feel awful."

Carella opened the door to his apartment.

"Teddy?" he called, and then he realized that calling her name was useless if she could not see his lips. He closed the door behind him and walked into the living room. He took off his jacket, threw it onto one of the easy chairs, and then walked through to the kitchen.

The kitchen was empty.

Carella shrugged, went back to the living room, and then opened the door leading to their bedroom. Teddy wasn't in the bedroom, either.

He stood looking into the room for several moments. Then he sighed, went into the living room again, and opened the window wide. He picked up the newspaper, kicked off his shoes, loosened his tie, and then sat down to read and wait for his wayward wife.

He was dog-tired.

In ten minutes, he was sound asleep in the easy chair.

Bert Kling was making a call on the company's time.

"How'd it go?" he asked Claire.

"It's too early to tell," she said.

"Did she read it?"

"Yes, I think so."

"And?"

"No expression."

"None?"

"None. She read it and said she would let my father know. Period."

"What do you think?"

"I think I love you," Claire said.

"Don't get mushy," Kling told her. "Do you think it'll work?"

"Time will tell," Claire said. "I adore you."

"I adore you, Chris," Priscilla said, "and I want to do this for you, but I just...don't...feel well."

"You'll feel better in a little while," Donaldson said. He paused and smiled. "Would you like some chewing gum?" he asked pleasantly.

"Call him, would you, Chris? Please, call him. Let's get this over with."

Call him, Teddy Carella wrote on the sheet of paper under the circles Chen had drawn. *My husband, Detective Carella. Call him. FRederick 7-8024. Tell him.*

"Now?" Chen whispered.

Teddy nodded urgently. On the paper, she wrote, *You must keep that man here. You must not allow him to leave the shop.*

"The phone," Chen said. "The phone is out front. How I can call?"

"Hey there!" Donaldson said. "Are you coming out?"

The beaded curtains parted. Chen stepped through them. "Sorry, sir," he said. "Slight delay. Sit a moment, please. Must call friend."

"Can't that wait?" Donaldson asked. "We're in something of a hurry."

"No can wait, sir, sorry. Be with you one moment. Promised dear friend to call. Must do." He moved toward the phone quickly. Quickly, he dialed. FR 7-8024. He waited. He could hear the phone ringing on the other end. Then…

"87th Precinct, Sergeant Murchison."

"I speak to Mr. Carella, please?" Chen said.

Donaldson stood not three feet from him, impatiently toeing the floor. The girl sat in the chair opposite the phone, her head cradled in her hands.

"Just a second," the desk sergeant said. "I'll connect you with the Detective Division."

Chen listened to the clicking on the line.

A voice said, "87th Squad, Havilland speaking."

"Mr. Carella, please," Chen said.

"Carella's not here right now," Havilland said. "Can I help you?"

Chen looked at Donaldson.

Donaldson looked at his watch.

"The…ah…The tattoo design he wanted," Chen said. "Is in the shop now."

"Just a minute," Havilland said. "Let me take that down. Tattoo design he wanted, in shop now. Okay. Who's this, please?"

"Charlie Chen."

"Charlie Chan? What is this, a gag?"

"No, no. You tell Mr. Carella. You tell him call me back soon as he get there. Tell him I try to hold design."

"He may not even come back to the squad," Havilland said. "He's—"

"You tell him," Chen said. "Please."

"Okay," Havilland said, sighing. "I'll tell him."

"Thank you," Chen said, and he hung up.

Bert Kling walked over to Havilland's desk.

"Who was that?" he asked.

"Charlie Chan," Havilland said. "A crackpot."

"Oh," Kling said. He had half hoped it was Claire, even though he'd talked to her not five minutes earlier.

"Guys got nothing to do but bug police stations," Havilland said. "There ought to be a law against some of the calls we get!"

"Was your friend out?" Donaldson asked.

"Yes. He call me back. What kind tattoo you want?"

"A small heart with initials in it," Donaldson said.

"What initials?"

"P-A-C."

"Where you want heart?"

"On the young lady's hand." Donaldson smiled. "Right here between the thumb and forefinger."

"Very difficult to do," Chen said. "Hurt young lady."

Priscilla Ames looked up. "Chris," she said, "I…I don't feel well…honestly, I don't. Couldn't we…couldn't we let this wait?"

Donaldson took one quick look at Priscilla. His face grew suddenly hard. "Yes," he said, "it will have to wait. Until another time. Come, Pris." He took her elbow, pulled her to her feet, held her arm in a firm grip. He turned to Chen. "Thank you," he said. "We'll have to go now."

"Can do now," Chen said desperately. "You sit lady down, I make tattoo. Do very pretty heart with initials. Very pretty."

"No," Donaldson said. "Not now."

Chen grabbed Donaldson's arm. "Take very quick. I do good job."

"Take your hand off me," Donaldson said, and he opened the door. The tinkle of the bell was loud in the small shop. The door slammed.

Chen rushed into the back room. "They go!" he said. "Can't keep them! They go!"

Teddy was buttoning her blouse. She scooped the pencil and paper from the tabletop and threw them into her bag.

"His name Chris," Chen said. "She call him Chris."

Teddy nodded and started for the door.

"Where you go?" Chen shouted. "Where you go?"

She turned and smiled at him fleetingly. Then the door slammed again, and she was gone.

Chen stood in the middle of his shop, listening to the reverberating tinkle of the bell.

"What I do now?" he said aloud.

She followed behind them closely. They were not easy to lose. He as tall as a giant, his blond hair catching the afternoon sunlight. She unsteady on her feet, his arm circling her waist, holding her. She followed behind them closely, and she could feel her heart hammering inside her rib cage.

What do I do now? she wondered, but she kept following because this was the man her husband wanted.

When she saw them stop before an automobile, she suddenly lost heart. The chase seemed to be a futile one. He opened the door for the girl and helped her in, and Teddy watched as he walked to the other side of the car. And then the taxicab appeared, and she knew the chase was not over, but that it was just beginning. She hailed the cab, and it pulled to the side of the curb, and the cabbie flicked open the rear door, and Teddy climbed in. He turned to face her, and quickly, she gestured to her ears and her mouth, and miraculously, he understood her at once. She pointed through the windshield where Donaldson was just entering his car. She took a long hard look at the rear of the car.

"What, lady?" the cabbie asked.

Again, she pointed.

"You want me to follow him?" The cabbie watched Teddy nod, watched the door of Donaldson's car slam shut, and then watched as the sedan pulled away from the curb. The cabbie couldn't resist the crack.

"What happened, lady?" he asked. "That guy steal your voice?"

He gunned away from the curb, following Donaldson, and then he glanced over his shoulder to see if Teddy had appreciated his humor.

Teddy wasn't even looking at him.

She had taken Chen's pencil and paper from her purse and was scribbling furiously.

He hoped she would not die in the car.

It did not seem possible or likely that she would, but he planned ahead for the eventuality, because if it happened, he didn't want to be caught short. It would be difficult getting her out of the car. This had never happened to him before, and he felt a tenseness in his hands as he gripped the wheel and navigated the car through the afternoon traffic. He must not panic. Whatever happened, he must not panic. Things had gone too well up to now. Panic could throw everything out the window. Whatever happened, he had to keep a clear head. Whatever happened, there was too much at stake, too much to lose. He had to think clearly and coolly. He had to face each situation as it presented itself. He had to face it and handle it.

"I'm sick, Chris," Priscilla said. "I'm very sick."

You don't know just how sick, he thought. He kept his eyes on the road and his hands on the wheel. He did not answer her.

"Chris, I'm...I'm going to throw up."

"Can't you—"

"Please, stop the car, Chris. I'm going to throw up."

"I can't stop the car," he said. He looked at her briefly, a side-glance that took in the pale-white face, the watery eyes. Roughly, he pulled a neatly folded white handkerchief from his breast pocket, thrusting it at her. "Use this," he said.

"Chris, can't you stop? Can't you please—"

"Use the handkerchief," he said, and there was something strange and new in his voice, and she was suddenly frightened. She could not think of her fright very long. In the next moment, she was violently ill and violently ashamed of herself for being ill.

"That guy's going to Riverhead," the cabbie said, turning to Teddy. "See, he's crossing the bridge. You sure you want me to follow him?"

Teddy nodded. Riverhead. She lived in Riverhead. She and Steve lived in Riverhead, but Riverhead was a big part of the city. *Where in Riverhead was the man taking the girl? And where was Steve? Was he at the squad? Was he home? Was he still out canvassing tattoo parlors? Was it possible he'd visit Charlie Chen again?* she wondered. She tore off a slip of paper, putting it with the growing pile of slips beside her on the seat. Then she began writing again.

And then, as if to check the accuracy of her first observation, she looked at the rear of Donaldson's car again.

"Are you a writer or something?" the cabbie asked.

It bothered Kling.

He got up and walked to where Havilland was reading a true detective magazine, his feet propped up on the desk.

"What'd you say that guy's name was?"

"What?" Havilland asked, looking up from the magazine. "Here's a case about a guy who cut up his victims. Put them in trunks."

"This guy who called for Steve," Kling said. "What'd you say his name was?"

"A crackpot. Sam Spade or something."

"Didn't you say Charlie Chan?"

"Yeah, Charlie Chan. A crackpot."

"What'd he say to you?"

"Said Carella's tattoo design was in the shop. Said he'd try to keep it there."

"Charlie Chen," Kling said, thoughtfully. "Carella questioned him. Chen. He was the man who tattooed Mary Proschek." He thought again. Then he said, "What's his number?"

"He didn't leave any," Havilland said.

"It's probably in the book," Kling said, starting back for his own desk.

"The hell of this thing is that the cops didn't tip to this guy for three years," Havilland said, wagging his head. "Cutting up dames for three years and they didn't tip." He wagged his head again. "Jesus, how could they be so stupid!"

"It looks like he's pulling over, lady," the cabbie said. "You want I should pull in right behind him?"

Teddy shook her head.

The cabbie sighed. "So where, then? Right here okay?"

Teddy nodded.

The cabbie pulled in and stopped his meter. Up ahead, Donaldson had parked and was helping Priscilla from the car. Teddy watched them as she fished in her purse for money to pay the cabbie. She paid him, and then she scooped up the pile of paper slips from the seat beside her. She handed one to the cabbie, stepped out, and began running because Donaldson and Priscilla had just turned the corner.

"What..." the cabbie said, but his fare was gone.

He looked at the narrow slip of paper. In a hurried hand, Teddy had written:

Call Detective Steve Carella, FRederick 7-8024. Tell him license number is DN1556. Hurry please!

The cabbie stared at the note.

He sighed heavily.

"Women writers!" he said aloud, and he crumpled the slip, threw it out the window, and gunned away from the curb.

Kling found the number in the classified. He asked the desk sergeant for a line, and then he dialed.

He could hear the phone ringing on the other end. Methodically, he began counting the rings.

Three…four…five…

Kling waited.

Six…seven…eight…

Come on, Chen, he thought. *Answer the damn thing!*

And then he remembered the message Chen had given Havilland: *He would try to keep the tattoo design in the shop.*

Jesus, had something happened to Chen?

He hung up on the tenth ring.

"I'm checking out a car," he shouted to Havilland. "I'll be back later."

Havilland looked up from his magazine. "What?" he asked.

But Kling was already through the gate in the slatted railing and heading for the steps leading to the first floor.

Besides, the phone on Havilland's desk was ringing.

Chen was walking away from the shop when he heard the telephone. He had left the shop a moment earlier, fired with the decision to go directly to the 87th Precinct, find Carella, and tell him what had happened. He had locked up and was walking toward his car when the telephone began ringing.

Perhaps there is no difference in the way a telephone rings. It does not ring differently for sweethearts making lovers' calls, it does not ring differently when it carries bad news, or when it carries news of a big deal being closed.

Chen was in a hurry. He had to see Carella, had to talk to him.

So perhaps the ring of the telephone in his closed and locked shop was not really so urgent. Perhaps it did not really sound so terribly important. It was, after all, only a telephone ring.

It was, nonetheless, urgent-sounding enough to pull him back from the curb and over to the locked door. It sounded urgent enough to force him to reach for his keys rapidly, find the right key, shove it into the hanging padlock, snap open the lock, and then throw open the door and rush to the phone.

It sounded urgent as hell until it stopped ringing.

By the time Chen lifted the receiver, all he got was a dial tone.

And since he had a dial tone, he used it.

He called FRederick 7-8024.

"87th Precinct, Sergeant Murchison," the voice said.

"Detective Carella, please," Chen said.

"Second," the desk sergeant answered.

Chen waited. He was right, then. Carella was back. He listened to the clicking on the line.

"87th Squad, Detective Havilland," Havilland said.

"I speak to Detective Carella, please?"

"Not here," Havilland said. "Who's this?" From the corner of his eye, he saw Kling disappear into the stairwell leading to the first floor.

"Charlie Chen. When he be back?"

"Just a second," Havilland said. He covered the mouthpiece. "Hey, Bert!" he shouted. "Bert!" There was no answer from the stairwell. Into the phone, Havilland said, "I'm a cop, too, mister. What's on your mind?"

"Man who tattoo girl," Chen said. "He was here shop. With Mrs. Carella."

"Slow down," Havilland said. "What man? What girl?"

"Carella knows," Chen said. "Tell him man's name is Chris. Big, blond man. Tell him wife follows. When he be back? Don't you know when he be back?"

"Listen—" Havilland started.

Chen impatiently said, "I come. I come tell him. You ask him wait."

"He may not even—" Havilland said, but he was talking to a dead line.

The girl was bent over double, the handkerchief pressed to her mouth. The tall, blond man kept his arm around her waist, holding her up, half walking her, half dragging her down the street.

Behind them, Teddy Carella followed.

Teddy Carella knew very little about con men.

She knew, though, that you could stand on a corner and offer to sell $5 gold pieces for 10¢, and you wouldn't get a buyer all day. She knew that the city was an inherently distrustful place, that strangers did not talk to strangers in restaurants, that people somehow did not trust people.

And so she had taken out insurance.

If she had a tongue, she'd have shouted her message.

She could not speak, and so she'd taken insurance that would shout her message, a dozen narrow slips of paper, with the identical message on each slip:

Call Detective Carella, FRederick 7-8024. Tell him license number is DN1556. Hurry please!

And now, as she followed along behind Donaldson and the girl, she began to shout her message. She could not linger long with each passerby because she could not afford to lose sight of the pair. She could only touch the sleeve of an old man and hand him the paper and then walk off. She could only gently press the dip into the hand of a matron in a gray dress and leave her puzzled and somewhat amused. She could only stop a teenager, avoid the open invitation in his eyes, and hand him the message. She left behind her a trail of people with a scrap of paper in their hands. She hoped that one of them would call the 87th. She hoped the license number would reach her husband. In the meantime, she followed a sick girl and a killer, and she didn't know what she would do if her husband didn't reach her, if her husband didn't somehow reach her.

"Sick…I…" Priscilla Ames could barely speak. She clung to the reassurance of his arm around her waist, and she staggered along the street with him, wondering where he was taking her, wondering why she was so deathly ill.

"Listen to me," he said. There was a hard edge to his voice. He was breathing heavily, and she did not recognize his voice.

Her throat burned, and she could only think of the churning in her stomach. *Why should I be so sick, why, why?*

"I'm talking to you, do you hear me?"

She'd never been sick in her life, never a day's serious illness. *Why, then, this sudden—*

"Goddammit, listen to me! You start throwing up again, I swear to Christ I'll leave you here in the gutter!"

"Wh...wh..." She swallowed. She was ashamed of herself. *The food, it must have been the food—that, and the fear of the needle. He shouldn't have asked me to be tattooed, always afraid of needles—*

"It's the next house," he said, "the big apartment house. I'm taking you in the back way. We'll use the service elevator. I don't want anyone to see you like this. Do you hear me? Can you understand me?"

She nodded, swallowing hard, wondering why he was telling her all this, squeezing her eyes shut tightly, knowing only excruciating pain, feeling weak all over, suddenly so very weak. "My purse, my purse, Chris, I've..."

She stopped.

She gestured limply with one hand.

"What is it?" he snapped. "What?" His eyes followed her gesture. He saw her purse where she'd dropped it onto the sidewalk. "Oh, goddammit," he said, and he braced her with one arm and stooped, half turning for the purse.

He saw the pretty brunette then.

She was not more than fifty feet behind them, and when he stooped to pick up the purse, the girl stopped, stared at him for a moment, and then quickly turned away to look into one of the store windows.

Slowly, he picked up the purse. His eyes narrowed with thought.

He began walking again.

Behind him, he could hear the clatter of the girl's heels.

"87th Precinct, Sergeant Murchison."

"Detective Carella, please," the young voice said.

"He's not here right now," Murchison answered. "Talk to anyone else?"

"The note said Carella," the young voice said.

"What note, son?"

"Aw, never mind," the boy replied. "It's probably a gag."

"Well, what—"

The line went dead.

A fly was buzzing around the nose of Steve Carella. Carella swatted at it in his sleep.

The fly zoomed up toward the ceiling and then swooped down again. Ssssszzzzzzzzz. It landed on Carella's ear.

Still sleeping, Carella brushed at it.

"87th Precinct, Sergeant Murchison."

"Is there a Detective Carella there?" the voice asked.

"Just a minute," Murchison said. He plugged into the bull's wire. Havilland picked up the phone.

"87th Detective Squad, Havilland," he said.

"Rog, this is Dave," Murchison said. "Has Carella come back yet?"

"Nope," Havilland said.

"I've got another call for him. You want to take it?"

"I'm busy," Havilland said.

"Doing what? Picking your nose?"

"All right, give me the call," Havilland said, putting down the magazine and the story about the trunk murderer.

"Here's the Detective Division," he heard Murchison say.

"This is Detective Havilland," Havilland said. "Can I help you?"

"Some dame handed me a note," the voice said.

"Yeah?"

"Said to call Detective Carella and tell him the license number is D-N-1556. Is this on the level? Is there really a Carella?"

"Yeah," Havilland said. "What was that number again?"

"What?"

"The license number."

"Oh. D-N-1556. What's it all about?"

"Mister," Havilland said, "your guess is as good as mine. Thanks for calling."

Kling sat in the squad car alongside the patrolman.

"Can't you make this thing go any faster?" he asked.

"I'm sorry, *sir*," the patrolman said with broad sarcasm, somewhat miffed with the knowledge that not too many months ago Kling had been a patrolman, too. "I wouldn't want to get a speeding ticket."

Kling studied the patrolman with an implacable eye. "Put on your goddamn siren," he said harshly, "and get this thing to Chinatown, or your ass is going to be in a great big sling!"

The patrolman blinked.

The squad car's siren suddenly erupted. The patrolman's foot came down onto the accelerator.

Kling leaned forward, staring through the windshield.

Charlie Chen leaned forward, staring through the windshield. He did not like to drive in city traffic. Doggedly, he headed uptown.

When he heard the siren, he thought it was a fire engine, and he started to pull over to his right.

Then he saw that it was a police car, and not even on his side of the avenue. The police car sped by him, heading downtown, its siren blaring.

It strengthened Chen's resolve. He gritted his teeth, leaned over the wheel, and stepped on the accelerator more firmly.

Carella swatted at the fly and then sat upright in his chair, suddenly wide awake. He blinked.

The apartment was very silent.

He stood and yawned. *What the hell time is it, anyway? Where the hell is Teddy?* He looked at his watch. She was usually home by this time, preparing supper. *Had she left a note?* He yawned again and began looking through the apartment for a note.

He could find none. He looked at his watch again. Then he went to his jacket and fished for his cigarettes. He reached into the package. It was empty. His fingers explored the sides. It was still empty.

Wearily, he sat down and put on his shoes.

He took his pad from his back pocket, slid the pencil out from under the leather loop, and wrote: *Dear Teddy: I've gone down for some cigarettes. Be right back. Steve.* He propped the note on the kitchen table. Then he went into the bathroom to wash his face.

"87th Squad, Detective Havilland."

"I wanted Carella," the woman's voice said.

"He's out," Havilland said.

"A young lady stopped me and gave me a note," the woman said. "I really don't know whether or not it's serious, but I felt I should call. May I read the note to you?"

"Please do," Havilland said.

"It says, *Call Detective Steve Carella, FRederick 7-8024. Tell him license number is D-N-1556. Hurry please!* Does that mean anything?"

"You say a young lady gave this to you?" Havilland asked.

"Yes, a quite beautiful young lady. Dark hair and dark eyes. She seemed rather in a hurry herself."

For the first time that afternoon, Havilland forgot his trunk murderer. He remembered, instead, that the Chinaman who'd called had said, "Man who tattoo girl. He was here shop. With Mrs. Carella."

And now a girl who answered the description of Steve's wife was going around handing out messages. That made sense. Carella's wife was a deaf mute.

"I'll get on it right away," Havilland said. "Thanks for calling."

He hung up, consulted his list of numbers, and then dialed the Bureau of Motor Vehicles. He gave them the license number and asked them to check it. Then he hung up and looked up another number.

He was dialing Steve Carella's home when Charlie Chen walked down the corridor and came to a breathless stop outside the slatted rail divider.

Steve Carella put on his jacket.

He went into the kitchen again to check the note, and then, because he was there, he checked the handles on the gas range to make sure all the jets were out.

He walked out of the kitchen and into the living room and then to the front door. He was in the corridor and closing the door behind him when the telephone rang. He cursed mildly, went to the phone, and lifted the receiver.

"Hello?" he said.

"Steve?"

"Yeah."

"Rog Havilland."

"What's up, Rog?"

"Got a man here named Charlie Chen who says your killer was in his shop this afternoon. Teddy was there at the time, and—"

"What!"

"Teddy. Your wife. She trailed the guy when he left. Chen says the girl with him was very sick. I've gotten half a dozen phone calls in the past half hour. Girl who answers Teddy's description has been handing out notes asking people to call you with a license number. I've got the MVB checking it now. What do you think?"

"Teddy!" Carella said, and that was all he could think of.

He heard a phone ringing someplace, and then Havilland said, "There's the other line going now. Might be the license information. Hold on, Steve."

He heard the click as the hold button was pressed, and he waited, squeezing the plastic of the phone, thinking over and over again, *Teddy, Teddy, Teddy.*

Havilland came back on in a minute.

"It's a black 1955 Cadillac hardtop," Havilland said. "Registered to a guy named Chris Donaldson."

"That's the bird," Carella said, his mind beginning to function again. "What address have you got for him?"

"41-18 Ranier. That's in Riverhead."

"That's about ten minutes from here," Carella said. "I'm starting now. Get a call in to whichever precinct owns that street. Get an ambulance going, too. If that girl is sick, it's probably from arsenic."

"Right," Havilland said. "Anything else, Steve?"

"Yeah. Start praying he hasn't spotted my wife!"

He hung up, slapped his hip pocket to make sure he still had his .38, and then left the apartment without closing the door.

Standing in the concrete and cinder block basement of the building, Teddy Carella watched the indicator needle of the service elevator. She could see the washing machines going in another part of the basement, and beyond that, she could feel the steady thrum of the apartment building's oil burner, and she watched the needle as it moved from numeral to numeral and then stopped at four.

She pressed the down button.

Donaldson and the girl had entered that service elevator and had got off at the fourth floor. And now, as the elevator dropped to the basement again, Teddy wondered what she would do when she discovered what apartment he was in, wondered, too, just how sick the girl was, just how much time she had. The elevator door slid open.

Teddy got in, pressed the No. 4 in the panel. The door slid shut. The elevator began its climb. Oddly, she felt no fear, no apprehension. She wished only that Steve were with her, because Steve would know what to do. The elevator climbed and then shuddered to a stop. The door did open. She started out of the car, and then she saw Donaldson.

He was standing just outside the elevator, waiting for the door to open, waiting for her. In blind panic, she stabbed at the panel with the floor buttons. Donaldson's arm lashed out. His fingers clamped on her wrist, and he pulled her out of the car.

"Why are you following me?" he asked.

She shook her head dumbly. Donaldson was pulling her down the hallway. He stopped before apartment 4C, threw open the door, and then shoved her into the apartment. Priscilla Ames was lying on the couch facedown. The apartment smelled of human waste.

"There she is," Donaldson said. "Is that who you're looking for?"

He snatched Teddy's purse from her hands and began going through it, scattering lipstick, change, mascara, and an address book onto the floor. When he came upon her wallet, he unsnapped it and went through it quickly.

"Mrs. Stephen Carella," he read from the identification card. "Resident of Riverhead, eh? So we're neighbors. Meet Miss Ames, Mrs. Carella. Or have you already met?" He looked at the card again. "In case of emergency, call…" His voice stopped. Then, like the slow trickle of a faulty waterspout, it came on again. "Detective Steve Carella, 87th Precinct, FRederick 7-802…" He looked up at Teddy. "Your husband's a cop, huh?"

Teddy nodded.

"What's the matter? Too scared to speak?" He studied her again. "I said…" He stopped, watching her. "Is something wrong with your voice?"

Teddy nodded.

"What is it? Can you talk?"

She shook her head. Her eyes lingered on his mouth, and following her gaze, he suddenly knew.

"Are you deaf?" he asked.

Teddy nodded.

"Good," Donaldson said flatly. He was silent again, watching her. "Did your husband put you up to following me?"

Teddy made no motion, no gesture. She stood as silent as a stone.

"Does he know about me?"

Again, no answer.

"Why were you following me?" Donaldson asked, moving closer to her. "Who put you on to me? Where'd I slip up?" He took her wrist. "Answer me, goddammit!"

His fingers were tight on her wrist. On the couch, Priscilla Ames moaned weakly. He turned abruptly.

"She's been poisoned, you know that, don't you?" he said to Teddy. "*I* poisoned her. She'll be dead in a little while, and tonight, she goes into the river." He saw Teddy's involuntary shudder. "What's the matter? Does that frighten you? Don't be frightened. She's in pain, but she hardly knows what the hell's happening anymore. All she can think about right now is her own sickness. Christ, it smells vile in here! How can you stand it?" He laughed a short, harsh laugh. The laugh was over almost before it began. His voice grew hard again. There was no compromise in it now. "What does your husband know?" he asked. "*What does your husband know?*"

Teddy made no motion. Her face remained expressionless.

Donaldson watched her. "All right," he said. "I'll assume the worst. I'll assume he's headed here right now with a whole damn battalion of police. Okay?"

Again, there was nothing on Teddy's face, nothing in her eyes.

"He won't find a damn thing when he gets here. I'll be gone, and Miss Ames'll be gone, and you'll be gone. He'll find the four walls." He went to the closet, opened it quickly, and pulled out a suitcase. "Come with me," he said. He shoved Teddy ahead of him, into the bedroom. "Sit down," he said. "On the bed. Hurry up."

Teddy sat.

Donaldson went to the dresser and threw open the top drawer. He began shoveling clothes into the suitcase. "You're a pretty one," he said. "If I came onto something like you…" He didn't complete the sentence. "The trouble with my business is that you can't enjoy yourself," he said vaguely. "Plain girls are good. They buy whatever you sell. Get involved with a beauty, and your secret's in danger. Murder is a big secret, don't you think? It pays well, too. Don't let anyone tell you crime doesn't pay. It pays excellently. If you don't get caught." He grinned. "I have no intention of getting caught." He looked at her again. "You're a pretty one. And you can't talk. A secret could be told to you." He shook his head. "It's too bad we haven't got more time." He shook his head again. "You're a pretty one," he repeated.

Teddy sat on the bed, motionless.

"You must know how it is," he said, "being good looking. It's a pain sometimes, isn't it? Men get to hate you, distrust you. Me, I mean. They don't like a man who's too good looking. Makes them feel uncomfortable. Too much virility for them. Points up their own petty quarrels with the world, makes than feel inadequate." He paused. "I can get any girl I want, do you know that? Any girl. I just flutter my lashes, and they fall down dead." He chuckled. "Dead. That's a laugh, isn't it? You must know, I guess. Men fall all over you, don't they?" He looked at her, questioning. "Okay, sit there in your shell. You're coming with me, you know that, don't you? You're my insurance." He laughed again. "We'll make a good couple. We'll really give the spectators something to ogle. We offset each other. Blond and brunette. That's very good. It won't be bad, being seen with a pretty girl for a change. I get tired of these goddamn witches. But they pay well. I've got a nice bank balance."

On the couch, Priscilla Ames moaned. Donaldson went to the doorway and looked into the living room. "Relax, lover," he called. "In a little while, you'll go for a nice refreshing swim." He burst out laughing and turned to Teddy. "Nice girl," he said. "Ugly as sin. Nice." He went back to packing the bag, silent now, working rapidly.

Teddy watched him. He had not packed a gun, so perhaps he didn't own one.

"You'll help me downstairs with her," he said suddenly. "The service elevator again. In and out, and whoosh, we're on our way. You'll stay with me for a while. You can't talk; that's good. No phone calls, no idle gossip to waiters, good, good. Just have to keep you away from pen and paper, I guess, huh?" He studied her again, his eyes changing. "Be good to have a ball for a change," he said. "I get so goddamn tired of these witches, and you can't trust the beauties. If you want to know something, you can't trust anybody. The world is full of con men. But we'll have a ball." He looked at her face. "Don't like the idea, huh? That's rough. It'll make it more interesting. You should consider yourself lucky. You *could* be scheduled for a swim with Miss Ames, you know. You should consider yourself lucky. Most women fall down when I come into a room. Consider yourself lucky. I'm pleasant company, and I know the nicest places in town. That's my business, you know. My avocation. I'm really an accountant. Actually, *accounting* is my avocation, I suppose. Women are my business. The lonely ones. The plain Janes. You're a surprise. I'm glad you followed me." He grinned boyishly. "Nice having somebody to talk to who doesn't talk back. That's the secret of the Catholic confession, and also the secret of psychoanalysis. You can tell the truth, and the worst that'll happen to you is twelve Hail Marys or the discovery that you hate your mother. With you, there's no punishment. I can talk, and you can listen, and I don't have to spout the love phrases or the undying bliss bit. You look sexy, too. Still water. Deep, deep."

He heard the sudden, sharp snap of the front door lock. He whirled quickly and ran into the living room.

Carella saw a blond giant appear in the doorframe, eyes alert, fists clenched. The giant took in the .38 in Carella's fist, took in the unwavering glint in Carella's eye, and then lunged across the room.

Carella was no fool. This man was a powerhouse. This man could rip him in two.

Steadily, calmly, Carella leveled the .38.

And then he fired.

April was dying.

The rains had come and gone, and the cruelest month was being put to rest. May would burst with flowers. In June, there would be sunshine.

Priscilla Ames sat in the squadroom of the 87th Precinct. Steve Carella sat opposite her.

"Will he live?" she asked.

"Yes," Carella said.

"That's unfortunate," she replied.

"It depends how you look at it," Carella said. "He'll go to trial, and he'll be convicted. He'll die, anyway."

"I was a fool, I suppose. I should have known better. I should have known there's no such thing as love."

"You're a fool if you believe that," Carella said.

"I should have known," Priscilla said, nodding. "It took a stomach pump to teach me."

"Love is for the birds, huh?" Carella said.

"Yes," she answered. She lifted her head, and her eyes behind the glasses glared defiance. But they asked for something else, too, and Carella gave it to her.

"I love my wife," he said simply. "It may be for the birds, but it's for the humans, too. Don't let Donaldson sour you. Love is the biggest American industry. I know." He grinned. "I'm a stockholder."

"I suppose…" Priscilla sighed. "Anyway, thank you. That's why I came by. To thank you."

"Where to now?" Carella asked.

"Back home," Priscilla said. "Phoenix." She paused and then smiled for the first time that afternoon. "There are a lot of birds in Phoenix."

Arthur Brown was conducting a post mortem.

"I couldn't figure why two big con men who are knocking over marks in the two-hundred- to a thousand-dollar category should bother with a little colored girl. Five bucks he got! He worked it as a single, without his partner, and all he got was five bucks!"

"So?" Havilland said.

"So it annoyed me. What the hell, a cop's got to bank on something, doesn't he? I asked Parsons. I asked him why the hell he bothered conning a little girl out of five bucks. You know what he said?"

"No, what?" Havilland asked.

"He said he wanted to teach the girl a lesson. Now, how the hell do you like that? He wanted to teach her a lesson!"

"We're losing a great teacher," Havilland said. "The world is losing a great teacher."

"You mustn't look at it that way," Brown said. "I prefer to think that the state penitentiary is *gaining* one."

On the telephone, Bert Kling said, "So?"

"It worked!"

"What!"

"It worked. She bought it. She's letting me go with my aunt," Claire said.

"You're kidding!"

"I'm dead serious."

"We leave on June tenth?"

"We do," Claire said.

"Yippppeeeee!" Kling shouted, and Havilland turned to him and said, "For Christ's sake, pipe down! I'm trying to read!"

The working day was over.

There was May mixed in the April air. It touched the cheeks mildly; it lingered on the mouth. Carella walked and drank of it, and the draught was heady.

When he opened the door to his apartment, he was greeted with silence. He turned out the light in the living room and went into the bedroom.

Teddy was asleep.

He undressed quietly and then got into bed beside her. She wore a fluffy, white gown, and he lowered the strap of the gown from her right shoulder and kissed the warm flesh there. A cloud passed from the moon, filling the room with pale yellow. Carella moved back from his wife's shoulder and blinked. He blinked again.

"I'll be goddamned!" he said.

The warm April moonlight illuminated a small, lacy, black butterfly on Teddy's shoulder.

"I'll be goddamned!" Carella said again, and he kissed her so hard that she woke up.

And, big detective that he was, he never once suspected she'd been awake all the while.

AFTERWORD

It's necessary that this be an afterword rather than an introduction because if it were placed *before* the book began, it would spoil the suspense—such as it is—of scenes you've now already read.

If you've been paying attention, you know that my original plan was to kill Carella at the end of *The Pusher*, which gleefully malignant intent was stifled by my misguided and greedy publishers who insisted that I could not kill a *hero*—who, by the way, had only appeared in one and a half books by then. *Some* hero!

Having had time to think over their suggestions while hanging in chains in the basement and being fed only bread and water—and never mind the brutal torture and such, which I am reluctant to describe in detail lest it cause vapors in those among you who are fainthearted—having had time, as I say, to reconsider the untimely demise of Stephen Louis Carella, to resurrect him, so to speak, I was now confronted with writing the next book in the series wherein this big *hero*, mind you, was to become a ☆☆☆ star ☆☆☆!!!

Recognizing the rarely disputed fact that behind all great men there stands a woman, it occurred to me that Teddy Carella—who had been invisible in the second book of the series and virtually nonexistent in the third book, wherein Carella should have lain down and died if he had a decent bone in his body—it occurred to me, as I say, that it wouldn't be a bad notion to revive Teddy

Carella, too, to give her a larger role in the proceedings, in fact, to have a sizable segment of the plot revolve around her. This was not too difficult a task to accomplish in that she had been conceived as someone both hearing- and speech-impaired, and therefore presumably more vulnerable to attack.

(Incidentally, as a point of perhaps minor interest, in these earlier books Teddy was called a "deaf mute." A reader pointed out to me some two or three years ago that this expression was now considered derogatory. Out the window it went, and Teddy is now speech-and-hearing impaired.)

As I say, it was easy to get Teddy in and out of trouble. More important, however, was fleshing out this wife of the ☆☆☆ star ☆☆☆ who—if Carella was to continue as the hero in subsequent books in the series—would have to play more than a mere supporting role. Have I mentioned that after the wild critical and public acclaim of the first three books (which sold fourteen copies each, including those purchased by my relatives), my greedy and misguided publishers decided to give me a contract for yet *another* three books, the first of which was to be *The Con Man*? If not, this was an oversight, and I beg your indulgence.

I don't know from whither sprang the notion of Teddy getting herself a tattoo. I feel positive that it preceded the idea of a killer tattooing his victims as a sort of calling card. I know that I still like the scenes between her and Charlie Chen—who makes a repeat performance many years later in *Ice*—and it's my continuing hope that a woman brave enough to submit to the torture of a tattoo needle (though nothing like what I suffered in that basement while my publishers were convincing me to bring Carella back to life) was a woman who could not, by the farthest stretch of the imagination, be considered "handicapped." I had never thought of Teddy as being handicapped, anyway, but it seemed to me that with the simple act of acquiring a tattoo, she achieved the heroic dimensions essential to the tracking of a killer, thereby elevating her to proper ☆☆☆ STARDOM ☆☆☆ alongside her big-hero husband.

As a final note of minor importance, I call your attention to the beginning of chapter 19, reproduced here as it appeared originally in the 1957 Permabooks edition:

> "Yeah. Start praying he hasn't spotted my wife!"
>
> He hung up, slapped his hip pocket to make sure he still had his .38, and then left the apartment without closing the door.
>
> **Chapter Nineteen**
>
> STANDING in the concrete and cinder block basement of the building, Teddy Carella watched the indicator needle of the service elevator. She could hear the washing machines going in another part of the basement, and beyond that she could hear the steady thrum of the apartment building's oil burner, and she watched the needle as it moved from numeral to numeral and then stopped at 4.
>
> She pressed the "Down" button
>
> Donaldson and the
>
> had got
>
> to th

If you are as careful a reader as the one who pointed out the error to me some years after the book's publication, you will have already noticed that in the second line of the opening paragraph, Teddy can *hear*. Yes. She *hears* the washing machines going, and she *hears* the steady thrum of the oil burner. (Be still, my thrumming heart!) Was this a miracle of modern science? No. It was simply the author's unfamiliarity with a character who was poised on the brink of celestial permanence. Which is to say, it was merely the author's *stupidity*, belatedly corrected in subsequent editions.

For those of you who wish to learn more about the impermanence of stardom and the fragility of fame, stay tuned for the introduction to *Killer's Choice*, coming soon to your local bar and grill, maybe.

Ed McBain

ABOUT THE AUTHOR

Photograph © Dragica Hunter

Ed McBain was one of the many pen names of the successful and prolific crime fiction author Evan Hunter (1926–2005). Born Salvatore Lambino in New York, McBain served aboard a destroyer in the US Navy during World War II and then earned a degree from Hunter College in English and psychology. After a short stint teaching in a high school, McBain went to work for a literary agency in New York, working with authors such as Arthur C. Clarke and P.G. Wodehouse, all the while working on his own writing on nights and weekends. He had his first breakthrough in 1954 with the novel *The Blackboard Jungle*, which was published under his newly legal name Evan Hunter and based on his time teaching in the Bronx.

Perhaps his most popular work, the 87th Precinct series (released mainly under the name Ed McBain) is one of the longest running crime series ever published, debuting in 1956 with *Cop Hater* and featuring over fifty novels. The series is set in a fictional locale called Isola and features a wide cast of detectives including the prevalent Detective Steve Carella.

McBain was also known as a screenwriter. Most famously he adapted a short story from Daphne Du Maurier into the screenplay for Alfred Hitchcock's *The Birds* (1963). In addition to writing for the silver screen, he wrote for many television series, including *Columbo* and the NBC series *87th Precinct* (1961–1962), based on his popular novels.

McBain was awarded the Grand Master Award for lifetime achievement in 1986 by the Mystery Writers of America and was the first American to receive the Cartier Diamond Dagger award from the Crime Writers Association of Great Britain. He passed away in 2005 in his home in Connecticut after a battle with larynx cancer.